Copyright © 2014

Rebecca R Sherwin

All Rights Reserved.

This book is a work of fiction. Characters, places, events and incidents are a product of the author's imagination. Any resemblance to real persons, living or dead, is purely coincidental.

Survival

I had the perfect life. No, really, I did.

I had everything I ever wanted.

I had a good job that paid the bills with enough money spare to eat out regularly and go on quarterly holidays in the sun.

I had a four bedroom detached house, a stone's throw from the countryside and just a ten minute drive to the city.

I had a car; I traded it in for a new model every two years. Before it needed an inspection or service, I had a shiny brand new one sitting on my double driveway.

I had a Rottweiler called Buster. Cliché, I know, but he was the final step. The one before you took the plunge and had a baby.

And I had the perfect man. We were happy and we were in love.

See? My life had finally fallen into place.

But little did I know that in my blissful state of ignorance, I was taking everything for granted. I didn't know my time in possession of perfection was running out.

I had no idea I was about to have everything ripped away from me. Again.

I didn't see it coming.

My name is Skye, and this is my story.

One

There has to be a way out. There has to be.
Almost autumn, 2002.

"Skye!"

My mother banged her fist on my bedroom door like she did every morning. Every. Morning.

I groaned and opened my eyes. I was in my third 'snooze' phase of the new day and I was not happy about being woken up before the fourth. Alarm clocks had snooze buttons for a reason.

"Skye!" she called again, and banged. Again. "If I have to listen to that alarm once more, you'll be investing in a new one!"

I groaned again and cursed. I did that a lot at home; I didn't want to be there. I hadn't for a long time; not since my father left to live with his new girlfriend and my life turned to shit. It was a day I would never forget. My mother stood by the kitchen window with her arms folded, looking out at the other houses in the cul-de-sac. My father packed his things and we watched from the sofa as he filled his car and pulled off the driveway. There was no conversation; we didn't get an explanation. He just said goodbye, in a voice that sounded nothing like the one he used when he told us he was proud of us, and he left.

We had a nice house when he lived with us. I had my own room with a big bay window. It's funny how you notice the little things when they're gone.

Living in a family home soon changed. My mother had never had a job and didn't even pretend to try and get one when he walked out. She let the government pay for everything and as a result, we had to move – to a two bedroom flat in a tower block.

It wasn't so bad, if you ignored the pounding music from the neighbours on one side and the suspicious smell of what the couple on the other side were smoking. Oh, and the old lady downstairs. She would bash the ceiling with her broom because she forgot she lived in a third floor flat provided by the council, instead of the bungalow she lived in with her husband before he died. She was nice enough, if you caught her on a good day, when she actually remembered her own name and what year it was.

I didn't hate my father; I didn't blame him for leaving. I only envied him for being able to escape. And I wished he had taken us with him… Us. My twin brother, Oliver, and me. I just wished he had run away with us both in tow.

My mother didn't care that we shared a room. I'm sure, at nineteen, it was illegal. The council didn't care and our mother didn't care enough to try to change it. Beth, our older sister…she got out two years earlier. She moved away to university and apart from the weekly call to make sure we weren't malnourished, she had her own life.

Oliver and I both held down two jobs so we could feed and clothe ourselves, and pay the water rates; we were two showers a day clean freaks. We worked all the hours we could, which was pointless because she only smoked and drank our money away. A vegetable or a hint of colour was a rarity in our fridge.

I was determined to get out, we both were. We decided one night, about five months in when we were high from inhaling next door's fumes, that we wouldn't put up with her for much longer. We would save enough money to move out and get a place together; a place with at least two bedrooms.

We only had each other. We had to stick together; keep each other sane and on the straight and narrow.

"Skye!" My mother's incessant banging and leechy voice continued.

I had turned the damn alarm off ages ago. I realised when she banged again and I considered getting out of bed, opening the door and banging my fist on her face to show her how it felt, that she didn't want me to be late for work. Less money on my paycheck meant fewer Marlboro Lights for her. I would go and earn the money, give her half and not tell her the other half would go into our savings box. Oliver and I would get out soon, I could feel it. Maybe it was the lingering smell of weed from the night before making me delirious, hopeful, when I should have known better than to have hope.

I heaved myself out of bed and looked across the room at my sleeping brother. He had pulled the duvet over his head to block out her voice so he could sleep before work. He had only been home from his other job for a couple of hours.

Marijuana effects or not, I had a feeling we would be okay. I had to keep that energy and channel it into making a better life for us. I could do that. What other choice was there?

But life doesn't work out the way you plan it, no matter how hard you try.

It's the unexpected we all fail to prepare for…

Two

How many Hulks does it take to celebrate New Year's Eve?
December 31st, 2002

    I managed to find myself some friends. I was convinced that if they knew the kind of life I lived, I would be a laughing stock, an outcast. Everyone had their own problems and were fighting their own battles; my job and the friends I made at work became a way to escape the kind of hell that waited for me at home.
    By day I worked at the local deli, putting together coffee orders and toasting panini and by night I operated the switchboard in a car insurance call centre. When I wasn't working, I sat in my room on guard in case my mother came snooping and found our savings, or I went for a few drinks with my friends. They knew little about me; they assumed I didn't get good enough grades to go to university. I could let them believe that. It was better than the truth. I hung out with Oliver and his friends, too. When I was with my brother I could pretend, just for a while, that we were part of a normal family again.
    I was on my way to meet Oliver after work when I thought about our father. He never came back like he said he would. I was nineteen, I wasn't stupid, but it hurt. He was a good father, as much as I knew what made a father good, but I had no idea why he left us. Deserting my mother I could understand; she was a hopeless drunk with no passion for life. Maybe Oliver and I did something wrong too. The thought plagued me constantly. After eighteen years he just decided he didn't want us anymore, and it hurt; more than having to go into a charity shop to buy something for the party. We were celebrating New Year's Eve with Oliver's friends and I was on my way there to meet him, wearing my charity shop dress with as much pride as I could.

I knocked on the front door and waited for an answer. It was a nice house, like the one we used to live in and I wondered if there were parents inside; parents who were still together and still taking care of their children.

A huge man with a dark tangle of hair opened the door and I almost shrieked in shock. Every inch of skin I could see was covered in ink. Tribal markings, symbols and script covered his neck and arms.

"Can I help you?" His voice was a deep baritone. I looked at the door number and then down at the piece of paper in my hand with the address on it. Oliver must have given me the wrong one.

My eyes danced between him and the address, but I couldn't stop my eyes lingering on him, in an almost blatant stare, studying his features. His big brown eyes sparkled with confidence, yet I could tell they were a barrier; for what, I didn't know. His smile was one-sided, a cocky smile that showcased a pair of full lips. There was something dangerously alluring about him.

"Miss?"

"Uh, sorry," I stuttered. "Is my brother here?"

"I might be able to tell you," he said with a hint of humour in that deep voice that drew my gaze from his powerful body up to his dark eyes, "if I know who your brother is."

I might have laughed, if it weren't for my discomfort. This guy was huge; I didn't know they made men in XXXL. I almost laughed again.

"Oliver. Oliver Jones."

"You're Ollie's sister?" He sounded surprised as he looked me up and down.

"I am."

"My apologies, ma'am," he grinned. "Come on in. You're missing the party."

He held the door open and I stepped in. The house smelled of polished wood and lemon. It smelled clean. It reminded me I had housework to do. I followed The Hulk through the house to a conservatory at the back. There were ten other men in there, including my brother, although I couldn't be sure of the exact number. I counted ten heads, but their bodies meshed into a sea of muscle. They were all huge. So was Oliver. How had that happened?

I didn't make a habit of checking my brother out but how had I missed *that*?!

"Hey, you're here!" He jumped up and squeezed me against him. He'd had at least three beers.

Beers three, four and five made him an affectionate – and now considerably bigger – teddy bear. Beer six onwards made him just want to sleep.

He handed me the rest of his bottle and presented me to the Hulk army surrounding us.

"This is Skye. She's my sister… She's off limits."

"Skye, the Skillet!" One of them roared and threw his tree trunk arms in the air.

"Skillet?" I turned my nose up. "You brought me here to cook for you?"

"Nah," the guy who opened the door said. "You're smoking hot and anyone who touches you gets burned."

I giggled. What a weird thing to say.

"Speaking of food…who's ordering pizza?" Another said.

Everyone ordered a pizza. One each. I guessed having muscles like The Rock gave you the appetite of a Blue Whale.

It was nearing midnight; the turn of a new year. The alcohol was making me reflective, while the others just got more excitable. It was strange, being surrounded by overgrown men who appeared to be the outcome of some sort of scientific experiment, but I was enjoying myself. I hadn't had real fun for a long time.

The year had been hell for Oliver and me. We were trying our best but we needed a break. Maybe the New Year would bring us some luck. Lord knew we needed it.

"So, Skillet," The guy I met first, who was called Cut Throat – clearly that wasn't his real name, but I didn't ask – brought my attention back. "Are you ready?"

"Ready for what?"

Before my question was answered, he switched the TV to the BBC, just as the countdown began and everyone stood up.

"Ten, nine, eight, seven, six, five, four, three, two, one. Happy New Year!"

Big Ben chimed and the fireworks went off in an array of colours that gave me intoxicated hope. Everyone clinked their bottles together and chanted like it was some sort of testosterone-fuelled ritual. I clinked my beer with them, but stayed quiet and let them do their thing.

Auld Lang Syne began and I grinned like an idiot. Before our family fell apart, the five of us would stand in a circle, cross our arms to hold hands and sing together.

'Should old acquaintance be forgot and nev-'

Before I had a chance to join in, a pair of strong lips met mine. When I gasped in horror, he took it as an invitation to shove his tongue in my mouth. He tasted of stale beer and smelled even worse. I lifted my hands and shoved him away and he flew back so fast I felt like my tongue had gone with him. When I opened my eyes, 'Slasher' was rolling on the floor with his hands over his face and Oliver was standing over him with clenched fists.

"Ollie," Cut Throat said cooly and Oliver's head flew in his direction. "No."

I was frozen to the spot as my brother instantly fell calm and obeyed Cut Throat. He stepped away, looked at me and spoke to the clear alpha of the group.

"Get him out," Oliver gripped my shoulders so tight I thought he would crush them, and checked me over. "Are you okay?"

"I'm fine," I reassured him. "It's fine. Forget about it."

The others had fallen silent; only the bang of the fireworks on the TV remained and Cut Throat and Slasher were gone.

"It's not fine," he barked. My brother had never been aggressive before and it worried me that something so small could get him riled up. "Party over, we're leaving."

They all apologised to me as we left to take the short walk home. I didn't know why they felt they had to, it was just a kiss. One I didn't want, but I didn't consider myself violated. I could have handled it.

Oliver threw his hoodie over my shoulders as we walked home. I wished we didn't have to go. I would have taken the taste of beer and the smell of sweat a hundred times over instead of going 'home'.

We arrived back and Oliver took his things to the bathroom to change. He knocked on the door when he came back.

"I'm ready," I called and met him at the door so I could use the bathroom.

That was our routine. He would change in the bathroom so I could have privacy and then I'd use the bathroom and return to get in bed.

It was his turn to check the savings so I stood by our door to make sure Mum didn't come in and he rummaged in the wardrobe for the shoe box. We didn't have much; five hundred and twenty six pounds, and a few coppers we didn't bother to count. It was a start; the seed that would soon blossom like the leaves on the tree outside my old bedroom. It was the beginning of our new life. Oliver nodded and gave me the thumbs up when he had put it back. I closed the door and we climbed in our beds.

"What was that about earlier?" I asked as I switched my nightlight off.

"Nothing," he said, turning his lamp off and I heard him get comfortable. "Go to sleep. I have an early start."

I turned over.

"Skye?"

"Hmm?"

"I love you."

"Love you too."

I listened to the sounds of celebrations echoing around the tower block as I closed my eyes and fell asleep.

Three

An eye for an eye makes us all blind...Or you're just blind because you're stupid.
  January 1st, 2003

Oliver had already left when I got up for work the next morning. I took a second, while I heard my mother hacking in the bathroom, to look at my brother's side of the room. It was bare, much like mine. We didn't have many possessions – a nightlight and beside cabinet each. He had left his bed unmade; he never did that. As I heaved my exhausted, overworked body out of bed and prepared to make Oliver's bed for him, my mother banged on the door and spluttered something about getting out of her house and not forgetting to bring her cigarettes back with me.

I shook my head and snarled with hatred for the woman who had raised me. She had no idea how relieved I was when I stepped out of the tower block and knew I would be free of her for a few hours.

The streets were quiet as I made my way to work. Saturday mornings were always quiet, but it felt eerie. It was freezing cold and the streets were lined with rubbish, discarded drink bottles and sick. I stepped past each puke patch holding my breath and took the short walk to the deli.

It was empty all day. A handful of people came in for coffee to try and battle their New Year's Day hangovers, but it was so quiet. Too quiet. Mark, the manager, tried to send me home but I refused. I couldn't spend the day with my mother knowing Oliver wouldn't be at home with me. And I couldn't skip a day's money. This year was our year and I wasn't going to start it a day's pay down.

Rebecca Sherwin

We didn't make much money, but we made enough. I picked up as many shifts as I could at the coffee shop and relied on the tips in the mug on the counter for extras. I only worked at the insurance place part time, ten hours a week, but it was something. Oliver worked at the metalwork factory in town, which earned him as much as both my jobs combined. He worked the odd evening at a gym, too, sweeping and mopping floors and cleaning the machines, to earn a bit more. The gym paid in cash.

We finally closed the coffee shop at 8pm. I was sure we spent more money staying open than we made, but I wasn't going to complain. I waited while Mark locked the door, said goodbye and made my way to the shop. I shoved my hands in my coat pockets to keep the cold away and walked further away from home. I had to buy Mum's cigarettes. I didn't want to talk to her but I knew I would have to if I went home without two fresh decks of twenty Marlboro's.
"Shit." I cursed when I saw the shop was closed. I ignored my shivering body and carried on to the next row of shops.
By the time I had found a shop, bought her cigarettes and made it home, it was 9.30. My stomach growled with hunger and my throat was dry from the crisp winter air. I grabbed a glass of water and stood at the sink.
"Did you buy my fags?" My mother skulked into the kitchen wearing the same clothes she'd worn all week.
She hadn't showered either. I could see the thick layer of grease that matted her once luscious golden hair. Her voice was hoarse and dry, ruined by smoking forty a day for the past year. The smoke from her last cigarette billowed up from the ashtray as she held her greedy hand out for the next supply. I threw the boxes on the counter, refusing to touch her, talk to her, or make eye contact.
I headed out of the kitchen, but she stopped me at the door.
"A man turned up for you," she croaked and shoved a piece of paper in my hand. "He wanted you to call him immediately... Don't bring your work home."
"Fuck you." I hissed and left the kitchen.
I wondered if she would have passed the message on if she knew it had nothing to do with money, although I had no idea who it was or what they wanted.

I shut my bedroom door, making sure nothing was out of place. I sighed in relief when it looked how I left it and flipped open my mobile phone. I dialled the number on the paper and waited.

"Hello?" A low voice crackled on the other end.

"Who is this?"

"Who's this?!" The man jumped on the defence.

"It's Skye. You turned up at my house."

"Oh, Skye! It's Curtis."

"Who?!"

He chuckled, "Cut Throat."

"Cut Throat Curtis?" I scoffed. What a name.

"That's me, Skillet. Are you at home?"

"Yes. Or I wouldn't be calling you."

"See? You burn."

I smiled, "What do you want?"

"I'm coming to pick you up. Be waiting outside in five."

He hung up and I stared at the phone for a minute. Odd. I quickly changed out of my uniform, grabbed my things and left. I didn't say goodbye to my mother. She had what she wanted; she wouldn't notice I was gone.

I waited outside in the cold for mere seconds before a beat-up little Volkswagen Polo screeched to a halt in front of me. No way. No way would a man Cut Throat's size fit in that car. But sure enough, as he wound the window down, I saw that he did indeed fit. And even left a little room for me.

"Get in, Skillet. It's freezing!"

I rolled my eyes and climbed in the car, warming my hands on the vents that furiously pumped hot air into the tin can I was sitting in.

"Where are we going?"

"It's your brother's big night," he answered as he set off down the road. "I'm taking you to see it."

"See what? What big night?"

"You haven't figured it out?" He looked at me but I shoved his face back in the direction of the road.

"Clearly not. Eyes on the road, Curtis."

"Easy," he laughed. "And it's *Mr* Curtis to you."

"I'm waiting."

"Slasher, Cut Throat? I thought you'd get it. Ollie is Juggernaut Jones."

"Why does he have a nickname?"

"Oh, Skillet," he shook his head and sighed. Patronising git. "We're fighters. Lovers, too. But that doesn't pay."

"What?!" I gripped the door handle and my body jerked in shock. "What?!"

"Calm down."

"My brother fights?"

"That's why he didn't want you there. I thought it was just 'cause it's the big one…Too late now."

I didn't think the car could get any smaller. It could, and it did. I was suffocating. My brother was a fighter. That wasn't okay. I thought he just swept the floor at Geoff's Gym. Naive, much? How the hell did I not see it?

Cut Throat – No, Curtis. I refused to call him his nickname when I knew why he had it – pulled up on an unlit road and killed the engine.

"Where is he?"

"In there," he pointed to a black door and I was out of the car before he could say anything else. I banged on the door furiously with both fists.

"Password," came a quiet voice as the door opened just a crack.

"Screw the password. My brother is in there."

"Password," is all the voice replied.

"I told you to wait," Curtis said from behind me.

"Password," the damn voice repeated.

"Row row row your boat."

The door opened and I looked at Curtis, dumbfounded.

"What kind of password is that?"

"Would you have guessed it?" He arrogantly cocked an eyebrow.

"No."

"Then, Madame, continue."

He smiled and nudged me over the threshold.

We climbed a set of dark stairs and then descended another set. Curtis opened a door at the end of an unlit hallway and led me into something that looked like a scene from a Rocky movie. Only there was a cage in the middle…

Survival (Twisted #1)

Four

I could have stopped it…If I'd have just opened my eyes, I could have stopped it…
January 1st, 2003

"Are you kidding me?!" I yelled over the thumping music as I watched the swarms of people around me. "This is really happening?"

"Yes, it's happening," Curtis held the top of my arm and led me towards the front, through the madness until we were at a table at the front, two metres from the cage. "Is it really so bad?"

"Yes!" I screeched, feeling more and more terrified by the minute.

There was so much noise. There were so many people. The excited energy buzzed in the air. The audience was getting a kick out of what was about to happen and then it hit me. We were in the thick of it. The night had already started; there had been previous fights, and there were more to come. The excitement grew with every second, telling me we were building up to something much bigger.

"Curtis?" I looked up at him as he held a chair out at a table for me and I sat down. He sat down next to me and my eyes never left him. "What did you mean about this being Oliver's big night?"

"Ah," he groaned and chewed on his thumb nail. "I don't know that I should tell you. You already look like you're about to spew. Water?"

"Spill it."

"The water?"

He was trying to be funny, the bastard. He'd brought me here, to the most terrifying night of my life and he was trying to be funny. I wanted to punch him. Hell, I was in the right place to do it.

"The truth, Curtis."

"I can't resist a pretty face," he said, waving at someone in the distance and mouthing that he wanted bottled water. He turned back to me. "It's the way this industry works. The bigger the fight, the more money. The bigger the win, the more sponsors next time you fight. Get it?"

I nodded.

"Like any area of the entertainment industry-"

"This is entertainment?"

"Wait 'til you feel the rush. You want the story or not, Skillet?" I nodded for him to continue. "The smaller fights go first. They go for five minutes in each round, a maximum of three rounds. You with me?" I nodded, speechless, "Championships and main events last for five rounds. The further on in the night, the bigger the profiles. People will stay for the main event, spend loads of cash, voila. The organisers made their moolah."

"Stop trying to be funny!" I shoved at him but he didn't even notice I'd touched him.

"I'm trying to make you feel better. Ollie has been a surprise mover up the ranks."

"Why is he fighting?" I asked, scanning the arena for my brother. I couldn't see him. I could usually feel him when we were close – twin sixth sense or whatever – but I couldn't feel him.

"For the same reasons we all do."

"Money? All this danger for money?"

"It's not dangerous if you do it right. This isn't pit fighting, Skillet," he chuckled, but I felt like a fish out of water. I had no idea what was going on. "And it isn't for money. It's for the rush, the release, the freedom, the passion. It's climbing the steps of that ring and standing in the middle to look at the crowd, knowing you and just one other are in control of your life for twenty-five minutes. During that time, nothing else matters."

I wanted to cry. I wanted to scream. I wanted to switch on the twin radar, find my brother and get him out of there. If he was doing it for release, there was only one thing he needed to escape from. Home. Me. We would find another way to solve it. I just had to find him.

"He's not here," Curtis said, causing me to stop looking at every face I could see. "He'll be in the back. Greasing up or shadowing," he continued when he noted my confusion. "Vaseline. Helps the punches slip off…and shadowing. Like a fight in slow motion. It's conditioning. He'll be fine."

"How can you know that?"

"He isn't called Juggernaut Jones for nothing."

My heart was racing. Nothing Curtis had told me made me feel one iota of comfort. My brother was about to get in a cage and fight. Fight. And there was nothing I could do to stop him. I was about to lose my cool, when the lights fell dim and the strobe lighting began. The music made me jump as it burst from the speakers. The drums of a post-hardcore band, accompanied by the scream of the male lead singer, bled out and filled the arena. My ears hurt and the aggressive music relentlessly attacking me only made my nerves amplify.

"Okaaaay!" the MC in the middle of the ring shouted. "Deep breaths…clenched fists…"

The audience chanted with him.

"Deep breaths…clenched fists. Deep breaths…clenched fists."

The MC continued, "Deep breaths, clenched fists, here comes Juggernaut Jones!"

I stopped breathing altogether as my brother jumped out, barefoot and topless wearing open fingered gloves, and I saw a bright green mouthguard in his hand as he raised his arms. He didn't look like my brother. Oliver was always the quiet one, the reserved one; the one more likely to stop a fight with carefully chosen words. No way would he walk out into a crowd of hundreds, ready and willing to punch a man. For fun. I didn't know who I was looking at as he walked the ramp, climbed into the ring and shook hands with the MC, but it wasn't Oliver Jones…It was Juggernaut Jones. Was it possible that he could have been both? I wasn't convinced. I was terrified. Beyond terrified. I was delirious and nauseas and my hands were locked so tightly together they hurt.

The other guy made his entrance. He was huge too. Couldn't Oliver have been up against someone who didn't match him muscle for muscle? More screaming from the speakers and I covered my ears with my hands, my eyes never leaving the other fighter. I didn't even catch his name. The MC's voice was drowned out by the screams, whistles and cheers of the people who had made their way forward and were now surrounding us. He bounced down the ramp and glared at my brother; he bared his teeth in a snarl and more screams erupted from the spectators. I turned my gaze to Oliver as he shook his arms and bounced from foot to foot. He was focussed, I could see that much. His eyes had glassed over and the small smile on one corner of his mouth told me he was confident. I thought I could feel it permeating from him to me. I must have been imagining it; making it up to ease my fear.

"Okay," the referee called and Oliver and the other fighter met him in the middle. "I want a good clean fight. I won't tolerate anything less. Are you ready?" he looked at Oliver, who nodded. He looked to the other guy, who nodded. It was happening. "Alright. Touch gloves, let's go."

They bumped gloves and backed up. The bell rang and they began to circle the ring, neither wanting to make the first move. The first guy swung his arm out and I held my breath as his fist passed Oliver's face. Oliver tried next, and missed. They edged closer and closer, until they locked hands behind each other's heads and tried to off the other's balance. I didn't want to watch, but I couldn't look away. In my peripheral, I could see Curtis on tenterhooks. One leg was bouncing and he was clenching his fists. He was nervous. He told me Oliver would be fine. Why was he nervous if Oliver was going to win?

The other fighter hit Oliver straight in the jaw. I raised my hand to my cheek; I could feel it. I was out of breath, my oxygen intake reduced the more Oliver exerted himself. They were on the floor, one trying to make the other submit and then they swapped. There was kicking and punching and flying fists. I couldn't keep up; I only knew that the first round felt a hell of a lot longer than five minutes. It felt like long, agonising hours of watching my brother fight. I didn't want it. Why would he want to do it? I got no rush; there was adrenaline, but the flight or fight response? I wanted to run and take him with me.

The same torturous routine went on for three rounds. Curtis comforted me in between, while Oliver was having Vaseline rubbed on a cut above his eyebrow and a load of water squirted into his mouth, but it didn't work. Nothing would work. I wouldn't feel better until I could slap some sense into my brother myself and make him promise he wouldn't do it again.

The fourth round started and my heart felt heavy. It felt too weighed down to beat. It was slow, but it was fast. It was heavy, but it was fluttery. I was a concoction of nervous anguish and I just wanted it to end.

"Knock him out, Ollie!" I cried. I just wanted it to be over.

The bell rang as the words left my lips and Oliver turned to find me. He didn't see the fist coming in his direction. His eyes connected with mine and a look of terror flashed across his face before the fist connected with the back of his head and sent him to the floor. His body went limp, his eyes closed. He didn't move.

Five

Twins. You're born together, you grow together, you learn together. You laugh together, you cry together…you fight together.
  And then what?
  January 1ˢᵗ, 2003

Oliver was unconscious before he was able to put his hands out to break his fall. His body slumped to the floor and my heart stopped as I watched it.

Time stopped. There was no bell.

Silence deafened the building.

The only movement was the referee standing over my brother and waving his arms in silent panic.

I couldn't breathe. I felt numb.

I took off towards the ring and launched myself at the cage. I could feel the cold metal; it was the only thing I felt. Cold.

Curtis wrapped his arms around my waist. I knew it was him; I could hear him shushing me. I could hear someone in the ring telling him to get me away. I was panicking. I was hysterical. I clung to the cage and watched as people dressed in black surrounded Oliver until I couldn't see him. I allowed Curtis to wrench me away but my body continued thrashing.

"You said he'd be fine!" I screamed when he set me down. I pounded his chest and repeated, "You said he'd be fine."

"I know."

I looked past him.

"No!" I cried, trying to get to Oliver as he was strapped to a stretcher. "No, no, no!"

"Skye, let them look after him"

"He needs me!"

Curtis lifted me off my feet and I stopped fighting. My body sagged as he threw me over his shoulder and made his way towards the exit. I silently sobbed as I was separated further from Oliver's lifeless body.

I sat in the waiting room surrounded by people, but I wasn't really there. I was still in the arena watching Oliver fall over and over again. All I could see was the pained expression on his face when his eyes met mine.

Curtis never let go of my hand, not once. But I didn't hold back. I couldn't.

Time ticked by; hours, minutes, I didn't know. All I knew was that with each agonising second that passed, my brother was somewhere in the hospital. Alone.

The door clicked open and I heard muffled voices as I continued to stare blankly at the floor.

"Skye…Skye…Skye," Curtis shook me and I looked up into the eyes of a doctor.

"Are you next of kin?" She asked. I nodded. "Are you his wife?"

I shook my head.

"She's his sister," Curtis answered for me and gave my hand a gentle squeeze.

"Where are your parents, Skye?" I just stared back at her, "Skye?"

"Unfit," I rasped. "Dad left, Mum is drunk. It's just us."

She nodded in understanding and turned to Curtis.

"Would you come with her to my office?"

Curtis stood and helped me to my feet. We reached the door before I stopped.

"I'm okay," I stepped away from him.

"But-"

"I said -- I'm okay."

I followed the doctor to her office and she shut the door behind us. She sat behind her desk and gestured for me to sit opposite. I stayed standing.

"I really think you should sit down, Ms Jones."

I relented and sat in the chair.

"My name is Doctor Khan. I'm in charge of your brother's care."

I continued to stare. I was close to breaking, to letting my heart shatter, but I had to keep it in. I had to be strong for Oliver.

"Are you sure you don't want someone here with you?"

I shook my head, "No. Thank you."

"Okay," she shifted in her chair and straightened her back. "It isn't good news, Ms Jones."

I choked on a sob and my bottom lip trembled. Oliver.

"Your brother suffered severe brain damage and he's no longer responding to any stimulus."

I shook my head again. She was lying.

"Right now, the ventilator is the only thing keeping Oliver alive, I'm afraid. A neurologist is due here shortly to confirm my diagnosis."

"Diagnosis?"

"Yes. The brain stem is what controls the flow of messages between the brain and the rest of the body as well as the vital functions such as breathing, heart rate, consciousness and awareness. Early indications show that Oliver's brain stem is no longer functioning."

I covered my mouth with my hand and my body trembled. The tears pooled and the pain plunged to every one of my nerve endings.

"Unfortunately, it is irreversible."

"No." I exhaled and couldn't breathe in.

"To confirm brain stem death, my colleague and I have to assess a specific set of criteria at least twice. We will then ask for your permission to cease mechanical ventilation."

I couldn't listen to any more. I stood up and paced the room. She was lying.

"Skye," she said, halting my pacing and stopping my incoherent mumbling. "It might be a good idea to start saying goodbye."

I stepped out of the office and looked around me. Nothing felt real. The bustling of the nurses at the station, the sound of a bottle falling inside the vending machine, a baby crying…nothing felt real. It felt like a nightmare. Not Oliver. She couldn't have been talking about my Oliver.

"Skye."

Curtis approached me and sensed it. His face fell and he took my hands in his.

"What did she say? When can we see him?"

I shook my head.

"We have to wait a while longer?"

I shook my head.

Curtis tried to laugh, but I knew he almost lost it, "What did she say?"

"He's dying," I keened and fell to the floor. Curtis fell too and stared at me. "He's already gone."

Six

And then...it ends. One twin dies and the other feels like she's lost half of her soul.
January 7th, 2003.

"My brother was a star. Not the kind that had fame and fortune, but the kind that brought light to the darkest corners of your life."

I stood on the pulpit at the front of the church. The pews were full; family, friends, his fighter friends. I didn't care about anyone in the room. Oliver was in a box behind me where he would spend the rest of eternity and there was more than a handful of people in attendance who could have prevented it, me included.

I cleared my throat and continued.

"He wasn't your average nineteen year old. He was kind, he was pure and he was my favourite person in the world. We were there for each other when no one else was. I only had nineteen years as his twin and I am grateful for every second. Today we bury Oliver before he had a chance to fall in love, before he could have a career, before he became a father. I choose to believe he's in a better place. I choose to believe he is watching over us and I know he would want us to be happy. I will carry Oliver's light with me, until I see him again, and I ask you all to do the same." I turned to the coffin. "Goodbye, brother. I love you."

I didn't know how I made it back to my seat, but I did. I didn't sit with my mother, father or sister; I sat in the last pew at the back on my own.

I stood alone at the front as Oliver's coffin was lowered into the ground. I didn't cry; I couldn't. I lost the ability to feel the day I lost the other half of me. I wasn't able to accept that he was gone.

I stared into the hole where my brother would rest, remembering the day I lost him. Our parents had turned up at the hospital eventually; my father with his new girlfriend hanging around him like a lost puppy and my mother had arrived with a bag big enough to smuggle in her bottle of vodka. I hadn't needed to smell the fumes emanating from her pores to know even the death of her eldest child and only son wouldn't have stopped her drinking. I had ignored them, refusing to acknowledge their presence, and stood by Oliver. I stroked his hair and committed his beautiful face to memory. If there was anything to be grateful for, it was that he looked like Oliver. The only indication that he'd been in a fight was the nick above his eyebrow. He looked relaxed; he looked ready. I stroked his cheek and held his hand. I told him everything would be okay as the beeps on the machine slowed and I let him go.

I hadn't cried in the hospital; I stayed strong for my brother and said my goodbye with strength and love in my voice as I desperately tried to conceal my heartbreak.

I had returned to the tower block alone the evening he died. I climbed in Oliver's unmade bed and cried until the exhaustion allowed me to slip into a tortured sleep.

I could hear someone calling my name as I replayed that day over and over in my mind.

"Skye?" Curtis brought me back to the present.

I realised I was alone at the grave as the earth was thrown into the hole. Everyone had left but Curtis. He took my hand, but I pulled away. I did it every time he tried to comfort me, which had been a lot in the past week, but I refused to accept it. And I refused to accept the pitiful looks from people and the "I'm sorry for your loss". It wasn't my life that had been lost; it was Oliver's. Mine had just gone with him.

It was my fault.

I shouldn't have sat in that arena and watched him fight. I shouldn't have distracted him by calling his name. For a split second his focus was lost and it cost him his life. Because of me.

It was my fault.

I should have done more than pour coffee and answer phone calls. If I had brought enough money in, if I had paid enough attention to the changes in him, he would have still been alive and not six feet in the ground. I refused to accept comfort when it was my fault my twin brother no longer had a life.

"Let's take you home."

Curtis wrapped his arm around me and refused to let me push him away as he led me through the graveyard and to his car.

"I don't want to go home," I said as he opened the door and helped me into the front seat. He crouched down next to me, but I kept my eyes on the trees ahead.

"Where do you want to go?"

I shrugged in response. He squeezed my knee, stood up, closed my door and walked round to climb in the driver's seat.

"What can I do?"

"Can you bring my brother back?" I still didn't look at him, but I saw him drop his head.

"No," he whispered, "but I can be here for you."

"Oliver should be here."

"I know."

He turned the key in the ignition and reversed out of the spot.

Seven

Life didn't stop, no matter how much I wanted it to. I had to go on living no matter how much it hurt.
January 10th, 2003.

I had to go to work. I had spent days locked in my bedroom consumed by fear. I was afraid to live without Oliver. I was afraid of the life that awaited me just outside the door. I was afraid of only having my mother, knowing she didn't want me. I was confused. I couldn't accept that Oliver was gone and although the fact was that he was never coming back, I sat on my bed and stared at the door, wishing he would burst through it and tell me it had been some sort of sick joke.

But he didn't come. Nobody did. I was alone and afraid of the future.

So I had to go to work. I mindlessly climbed in the shower, welcoming the burn of the hot water as it seared my skin, reminding me that I was living a nightmare. I scrubbed myself dry with the cleanest towel I could find and pulled on some clothes. I didn't know what I put on; I was on auto-pilot, completely disconnected from everything. I just wanted it to go away. The pain. The regret. The ache that told me there was a hole in my heart that would never be filled. I wanted to forget it all, I just didn't know how.

I pulled on my coat and left the silent, dark flat. My mother was home, I could see the light from her room under her door as I left, but she didn't come out.

I walked the dark streets alone with nothing but my thoughts to keep me company. Thoughts that weren't welcome.

I got to work and sat at my desk and pulled on my headset. I logged onto the system and looked around me as it set up. I didn't need to see them looking at me. I could feel it.

Every pair of eyes in the room were on me. Eyes full of sympathy and pity. I didn't know any of them; we just worked in the same call centre, but Oliver's death had made the local news and it was immediately obvious that all of the eyes had read about the accident. That's what they called it; an accident. It wasn't accident, it was a tragedy and my fellow phone operators were looking at me like I was hot gossip.

"You should take a picture. It'll last longer," I said, watching as they all hid behind their computer screens.

"I'm sorry for your loss," the woman in the seat next to me reached out and squeezed the top of my arm.

I nodded and bowed my head, shielding my eyes with my hand to hide the burning tears that threatened to stream from my eyes. The beep in my ear alerted me to my first call.

"Good evening, Lindan Insurance. Can I take your name and policy number, please?"

I worked my shift, blocking out the sensation of being watched and the sound of whispers between calls. I kept my mind on the shoe box in my wardrobe, tucked away in Oliver's drawer. That box, and what was in it, was my only hope. My only chance of escape. I kept my head down and ignored the unwanted attention, focusing on that goal.

It was pointless; I felt like I was losing it. My anger grew. My frustration intensified and I felt more and more out of control with every minute that passed on my computer screen and every customer who called and expected me to move mountains because they'd crashed their car.

What was the point? What was the reason for any of it? Money didn't matter. My job didn't matter. The people sitting around me waiting for me to break down didn't matter. They weren't going to get it. I was stronger than that.

I finished my shift and left, walking home alone.

I climbed in bed, covered my face with my pillow and screamed. I screamed until my throat was sore and then stared out of my window at the night sky as the tears rolled down my face, wondering what the hell I was going to do with my life.

Eight

Sometimes, the only way to punish yourself is to let someone in.
February 7th, 2003.

It had been one month. One month that already felt like a lifetime of solitude. I ended up quitting both my jobs – there was no point in working when I had nothing to work for. I was ashamed, but I had given up. I ignored calls from my friends; they were no longer friends. How could I spend time with people when they pointlessly tried to make me feel better about something they didn't understand? Oliver no longer had friends. The fighters at Geoff's Gym sent me flowers every week with a note telling me they were thinking of me and I was welcome at any time. The flowers went straight in the bin; flowers die, just like my brother did. I stopped eating too. I didn't have enough money to buy food since I quit work and the woman who gave birth to me didn't buy any. She sat in her bedroom, only coming out to go and buy vodka and cigarettes. I never saw her. Dad disappeared again, much like he had when the ball got rolling, no doubt to seek comfort from his girlfriend. Beth called every day for the first week, offering to move in. I told her to move on, to stay where she was. She had to make something of herself and make Oliver proud.

I continued to sit in my room and stare at everything Oliver and I had. None of it mattered anymore. I slept in his bed every night and told him I loved him before I closed my eyes and the nightmares took over. They were the only things that reminded me what was happening. The images of my brother in his final hours would forever be etched into my mind and remind me that I had failed.

Curtis became the only constant in my life. He found us a park not far from home and he took me there every day to look out at endless fields. Sometimes there were children in the playground and I imagined how Oliver would have been as a father. He would have been perfect. But mostly, the park was empty and we just sat in silence.

It was a cold day. I sat on the picnic table wrapped up in my coat and the patchwork blanket Curtis put over me. He blew on his hands and shoved them in his coat pocket.

"Here."

I slid closer to him and gave him half the blanket. He moved closer still, wrapped his arm around me and pulled the edges of the blanket together so it closed around us.

"I'm sorry," he said, so quietly his voice was almost lost to the raindrops that began to fall slowly to the grass. "I'm so sorry."

I shook my head.

"Oliver wouldn't have been there if it wasn't for me," he continued.

"That's not true," I let a few tears fall and watched as they got lost in the rain. "I guess everything that happened before led him to you. You couldn't have stopped him."

"I could have tried."

"You didn't know this would happen."

"But the fact that it *could* happen should have been enough."

"Stop," I said, resting my head on his shoulder. "Oliver wouldn't blame you."

"I blame me."

"I blame me, too. It doesn't bring him back."

We sat in silence as the rain continued to fall. We didn't care; we stayed in the same spot until darkness fell and we were soaked.

"Can I take you somewhere?" Curtis asked as he helped me off the table.

"Where?"

He didn't answer. He took my hand and led me to the car.

I didn't expect Geoff's Gym to look like it did. I didn't know what I expected; I never got the chance to see where Oliver spent his days. It was a small building in a car park, light and inviting. It wasn't bathed in the darkness I expected when I thought about fighting.

"Why are we here?" I asked as we climbed out of the car.

"I live here," Curtis pulled out a set of keys and opened the front door. "My parents deserted me too."

I hesitated on the threshold, but it was where Oliver had spent his time. It was the last connection I had to him. I stepped inside and Curtis locked the door behind us.

The oxygen was squeezed from my lungs as I looked around. There was a ring in the middle, but I quickly looked away from it as the blade of grief twisted in my chest. There was a group of punchbags hanging from the ceiling on one side and some weight-lifting and training equipment on the other. I could feel Oliver; his presence was absorbed into the eggshell paint on the walls and it enveloped me in longing.

"We all feel him," Curtis said noting my reaction, and led me towards the far end of the gym. "It's like he's still here. I haven't been able to train since - but I feel him."

"He liked it here?"

"Loved it," he unlocked another door and we stepped into a hallway. "This place is like a second home to most of the boys. Geoff looks after us."

"I'm glad he was happy here."

We climbed a staircase and stepped onto an open living area. It was small and dark and smelled of Curtis. I never noticed he had a smell before, but I noticed it then. It was comforting.

"I wish he would have brought you here."

"Why? I can't fight."

He took two bottles of water out of the fridge and handed one to me.

"You wouldn't have to. But you could have escaped, too," he gave me a sorrowful once over. "Wait here."

He disappeared into a room and came back minutes later with some clothes. He had changed into a pair of lounge trousers and a t-shirt and handed me a pile of similar things.

"You can change in the bathroom," he pointed to another door. "I'll dry your clothes."

"Will you tell me a story?"

We were sitting in silence on his worn brown leather sofa, listening to the whirring of the dryer.

"What kind of story?"

"Any kind. I just want to hear your voice."

I didn't think I needed a friend, but I did. I could talk to Curtis and know he understood. I didn't have to tell him about my life, he already knew. I didn't have to pretend everything was okay because he knew it wasn't. He shared my pain. He loved Oliver too.

"Once upon a time," he started and shifted closer, "there was a boy. He was a happy boy. He played football on Saturdays and his father always told him he would be a star. His favourite dinner was sausages and mash. His mother cooked it for him before she went out with his father. It was their anniversary and the lady next door came over to build jigsaws with the boy and put him to bed. The boy was five and he loved the Teenage Mutant Ninja Turtles.

"They built the puzzle and the lady tucked him up in bed and read him a story. The boy fell asleep and dreamed of the porridge his mummy would make him for breakfast, but the lady was still there when he woke up. She made him toast with strawberry jam. He didn't like jam, he liked porridge and honey. The lady looked sad so the boy ate his toast and sat on the sofa with her to watch TV."

I closed my eyes and rested my head on his shoulder. I heard the pain in his voice and my heart broke for him.

"The boy's mummy and daddy never came home. Their car broke on the way back and the angels took them to keep them safe."

"Curtis."

"Shh," he looked into my eyes and stroked his thumb over my chin. "Just listen."

I pursed my lips and he continued.

"He stayed with his aunt for a while but he wasn't nice to her. He didn't want an aunt-mummy, he wanted his mummy. As he got older, he got angrier. He didn't understand why his friends had their parents and he didn't. He used to fight, but he would lose because he couldn't control his anger."

He wrapped his arm around me and pulled me closer as I cried and his grief became palpable. As it swirled around us, our connection deepened and we shared the pain. We shared the relief of having each other.

"One day, when he was fifteen, his aunt packed his things in a bag and drove him to a little building on the outskirts of town. He met Geoff. Geoff was short and fat and had a weird cockney accent. He took the boy's bag and led him upstairs. He showed him a little flat and told the boy he could have it for free if he kept it tidy, mopped the floor of the gym and learned how to fight properly.

"He put the kettle on and turned to the boy. "I'm going to help you with the pain, Curtis." He said, "I'm going to teach you how to turn it into power. I'm going to train you to be a great man."."

He stopped talking and stared at the wall opposite.

"And…?" I asked.

"And then the dryer stopped," I looked at him confused, but he smiled at me and all hint of the hurt I heard in his voice disappeared. "Our clothes are dry."

Nine

Sometimes hope is all you have.
February 14th, 2003

Valentine's Day. I hadn't yet reached a point in my life where I would get excited about such a day. My father would buy me a card when I was a kid, with a teddy bear and packet of Love Heart sweets, but I'd never had a real boyfriend. It was all alien to me; boy meets girl, girl swoons and loses her tongue, boy woos girl until she is powerless to his charm and then they become inseparable. In the blink of an eye, two lives become one. It was a great idea, a beautiful romance that would stand the test of time, but that's all it was. Idealism. It wasn't real. And I had no idea how to talk to members of the opposite sex without getting tongue-tied and looking like I'd never had a day's schooling. It didn't matter, really. I was convinced it wouldn't happen for me. I was content with watching it in movies while I gorged on ice cream to try and stick it to my depression.

My mother had a date. It was the only thing she had spoken to me about for weeks. I'm sure she told me just to gloat – the forty year old drunk could get a date, but her nineteen year old daughter would be at home, simultaneously shoving popcorn and spoonfuls of Nutella in her mouth.

I felt sorry for any man walking into the eye of that storm. My mother was a ticking time bomb; the poor fool had no idea what he was getting into but I had no intention of warning him. She was his problem now. Good luck to him.

I stood in the kitchen, microwaving my popcorn when she walked in. The buttery smell of my popcorn mixed with the smoke from the cigarette that hung from her lips made my stomach turn. At least she had washed her hair. Maybe her date enjoyed making out with an ashtray.

She pulled a little bottle of cheap vodka from the cutlery draw and downed it in one.

"Dutch courage," she shrugged and grinned, showcasing her decaying teeth. I was ashamed to be related to her. "Have a wonderful Valentine's."

I watched as she left. I didn't tell her she had the bottom of her dress tucked into her knickers.

My evening was as uneventful as every other day. I'd wake up, spend the day with Curtis if he wasn't working, participate in life as much as I had to, and sleep. Sometimes I spent evenings with Curtis, but he was a serial dater. At least, I thought he was. I saw the looks from women, and the tender side I had caught a glimpse of made him quite a catch.

I was busy watching a movie and eating Nutella, sucking every trace of it off the spoon after each mouthful, when there was a knock on the door. I forced myself off the sofa and looked through the peephole. Curtis. *Sweet Jesus.* I scrubbed my finger over my teeth to remove all evidence of my pathetic night in and opened the door.

"Happy Valentine's Day," he smiled and held out a single red rose.

"What's this for?"

He shrugged, "Ollie wouldn't want you alone on the one night you're supposed to be shown how special you are."

Oliver. It was easier to talk about him, especially around Curtis. We weren't at the sharing anecdotes point; the pain was too raw, but we reminded ourselves why we had each other.

"Thank you."

"You can't go out dressed like that," he nodded towards my old pyjamas and I noticed he was in jeans and a shirt. I didn't think they made Hulk sized button-ups. "You've got five minutes."

I didn't ask questions. I scrambled to my room and changed into the nicest jeans I had, paired with the pink blouse I wore when I graduated college. I was surprised it still fit – the Nutella had been nicer to me than I deserved.

I pulled the only bag I owned over my shoulder and took some money from the shoe box.

"Wow. That was quick," Curtis looked at his watch as I returned, and opened the door for me.

"Why don't you have a date tonight?" I asked as we sat at our table in the restaurant.

"I do. You're my date."

I laughed, "This isn't a real date."

"Of course not," he shifted and half-filled my wine glass.

"So where's the harem?"

"I gave them a break," he winked at me and picked up his menu.

I picked up mine, but couldn't concentrate on the words. Curtis carried his pain well. I knew he harboured as much as me, if not more, but you couldn't tell. Anyone who looked at me could tell I was a finger snap away from falling apart, but Curtis was a soldier. I had a feeling I had only reached the tip of the iceberg when it came to his sorrow, but I would only know about it if he told me. His poker face was incredible; I needed to work on mine. Maybe then he wouldn't feel he needed to hang around me while I floated through life and he could make something of himself. Geoff had already made him a great man, he was destined for greater things than hanging around and babysitting me.

"Skye?" I looked up to see Curtis and the waitress waiting for me to order.

"Spaghetti bolognaise, please," I ordered the only thing I knew would be on the menu. I hadn't even looked.

My father used to make a great bolognaise.

I had never been drunk before. I tended to steer clear of alcohol, knowing what it did to my mother. Even when I had gone out with the few friends I had, I didn't drink much. A glass of wine was enough for me, but Curtis and I shared a few bottles of wine over dinner while we talked. Hours passed in no time and I noticed the effects of the drink as I stood in the bathroom and washed my hands. I didn't know what kind of drunk I was. Was I the giggly kind? The kind that got aggressive? Or was I going to break down and cry and cover Curtis in snot? I had no idea, but I waited in the bathroom for a while and splashed my face with water to try and sober up. It only made my mascara run and I looked worse than before. I sighed, giving up on concealing my state, and left.

Curtis was waiting for me at the table and handed me my coat and bag. I rummaged to find some money, but he closed his hand around mine.

"It's paid."

"I can pay for my dinner," I argued. Maybe I was an argumentative drunk.

"I know. But it's done. The cab is outside."

He took my hand and we both ignored the way I jumped at the contact as he led me outside and helped me into the car.

"Geoff's?" I asked as the cab pulled up outside the gym. Curtis paid the fare and we climbed out.

"I don't want you to be alone," he said, working to unlock the door. "You can have my bed, it's clean. I'll sleep on the sofa. I just don't want you to be on your own tonight."

"Thank you."

I staggered in through the door and stopped just inside. The gym was dark, only the lights above the ring remained. They illuminated the ring in bright white light and left everything else in shadow. I dropped my bag and coat, and walked towards it. Circling the ring, I ran my hand along the edges of the canvas, and then the bottom rope. There was just something magical about it. It must have been the wine talking, but I knew why Oliver loved it and I was beginning to see why Curtis did too. I turned to find him looking at me.

"Will you show me?" I asked as he walked slowly towards me.

"Show you what?"

"What it feels like to be free."

He stopped in front of me and stared. I waited for him to say something, anything, but he didn't. I giggled; because of the wine, because of his reaction; I didn't know but the giggling made me sway. The sway gave my feet a life of their own and I tumbled sideways until my arms were wrapped around a poor, unsuspecting punchbag. It swung a little from the chain connecting it to the ceiling. I went with it until Curtis stopped the swinging and halted my giggling with a similar look to the one he gave Oliver on New Year's Eve.

"Let go."

My arms fell to my sides and I sat on the floor.

"I miss him," I fought back the tears as he sat opposite me.

"I know."

"I really miss him, Curtis. I'm alone and I don't know what I'm doing anymore."

"You're not alone," he smiled weakly. "You've got me and we'll find your path together."

I couldn't respond. I just stared at the floor.

"You will be okay, Skye," he rested his hands on my knees. "If you want me to help you, I will. I'll show you a few things, but promise me something?"

"What?"

"You'll never get in that ring...this one or any one."

"Why?"

"Just promise me."

"I promise," I nodded. "I promise."

"Thank you."

He leaned over and kissed my forehead. I grabbed his wrists before he pulled away and closed my eyes as he kissed the bridge of my nose, then the tip. One eye, then the other. One cheek, then the next, and finally his lips gently touched the corner of my mouth. He moved over my lips to the other corner and I released a sigh. He sat back and I opened my eyes.

"Come on," he stood up and helped me to my feet. "It's getting late."

My steps slowed as I walked behind him, watching the way his muscles rippled beneath his shirt. He walked with purpose, like he was on a mission, like he was fighting something...or fighting *for* something. He was going to help me and I was going to let him. One large hand reached back for me and I set my hand in his, watching as his fingers cocooned mine and I hoped I would find my fight, too.

Ten

The attraction hit me like a right hook…and it stung like a hive of bees.
February 15th, 2003.

"Okay, first lesson. Stance," Curtis said. We were in Geoff's gym and I was standing in front of a punchbag. "Don't stand like a girl."

He had arranged some sports clothes for me, a pair of black shorts, a white t-shirt and thin-soled lace-up boots.

He shoved a pair of boxing gloves on my hands, black ones. They were lighter than I thought they would be and I flexed my fingers.

I thought I looked the part, but obviously I didn't. I was standing like a girl. What did that even mean?

"What does a girl stand like?"

"That," he nodded at me with a hint of a smile. "Weight on one leg, hands on hips. Balance your weight evenly."

I dropped my arms and stood up straight. Curtis bent down and pulled one foot forward. He stood up and pushed down on my shoulders so my knees bent.

"Bounce." I raised my eyebrows at him. "You have to be light on your feet. You don't bounce while you fight, it burns energy, but do it now. Feel how light you need to be."

I bounced from one foot to the other, "Like this?"

"Just like that,"

I was impressed he kept his eyes on mine, although secretly, I wouldn't have minded if he lowered his gaze slightly.

"Keep going. Right or left handed?" He grabbed my gloved hands and lifted them up. I nodded to my right hand and he pushed it back. "Dominant hand goes back."

He pushed the creases of my elbows so my hands came up in front of my face. I liked having his hands on me, but it was hard to focus and take in what he was telling me, and keep bouncing, with him so close.

Curtis took a step back to look at me. His eyes darkened; it was a dangerous look that almost made me stop and kneel before him. What was wrong with him? His eyes had turned to a chocolate storm and his arms came up, folding over his chest. I didn't know if he was angry; I thought maybe I wasn't bouncing properly. I concentrated on being light but I felt weighed down by the tension that had consumed him. I saw it, as his eyes moved over every inch of my body, leaving a burning trail that made me feel like marked territory: it was the gloves, the fight. His eyes kept returning to the ominous black leather that my hands were encased in; whatever he was thinking was torturing him. My instincts were telling me to go to him, to comfort him, to clear his mind in whatever way he needed, but as I prepared to go with my instincts, he spoke.

"Once you start, you can't stop," he said, his eyes glassed over. "You have to battle on forever. From this moment on, there's no excuse to give up. You have to believe you can do this before I can teach you how."

"I'm ready, Curtis," I breathed as his eyes fell on mine. I held my ground. "I'm ready to fight."

A shiver rippled through him and I watched his eyes change; they lightened. He had returned from wherever his mind had taken him.

"Stop bouncing. Dip your chin, look over your gloves," he watched me intensely as I did, and smiled softly. "You look cute."

I gasped, "Uh…"

"The most important lesson is to relax. And breathe," he patted my back and I let out the breath I was holding.

"Got it," I sighed. "Breathe."

"Good. Now, jab."

"What?"

"Jab."

"What the hell is jab?"

He squeezed the bridge of his nose but smiled, "I've got my work cut out. It's a simple punch with your left hand. The most important punch in boxing."

He moved my left hand slowly as he explained it to me.

"Keep your body still, just straighten your left arm. Turn your fist so your hand is palm down and exhale."

He let go and I tried on my own. I noted his smile as my fist connected with the punchbag. It felt good.

"Again," I did. "Good. Again, but with power. Exhale sharply, focus on your breathing. Stay relaxed, just tighten your fist as you punch."

He watched as I continued to punch the bag, keeping his eyes on my hands and adjusting my posture when I let it slack. I was enjoying it; I wasn't doing much, but I enjoyed it a lot more than I thought I might.

"You're doing good. Another?"

"Yes."

"Okay, the right straight. Your strongest punch," he stepped round to the other side of me and extended my right arm like he did with my left. "With this one, you need to pivot."

"How?"

"Like this," I jumped as he placed one hand on my hip, the other on my shoulder, and turned the top half of my body. I had the sudden urge to close my eyes and savour his touch. I did, just for a second but the coolness in his voice made me rethink and open them again. "Same as before, but move your body into it. Keep going."

I was soon doing it by myself, but Curtis set his hands on my hips and that's where they stayed. I let the power I felt from him move through me until I was worn out. I was breathless, shaky and hot from the warmth of his hands cupping my hips and applying gentle, intoxicating pressure. I stopped punching and closed my eyes without thinking, to concentrate on the feel of him so close. I enjoyed it more than I should have; I was heady, floating, fuzzy.

I held my breath when his lips whispered over my shoulder and a whimper escaped when he kissed the crook of my neck.

"I think that's enough for today," he let go of me and stepped back.

"But-"

"I'm hungry. Are you hungry? Let's eat."

I watched him disappear out the front door of the gym as a couple of fighters made their way in.

***

Curtis taught me a few moves and how to put them together over the next couple of weeks. It was nothing like what I saw the other guys doing. Their tricks were fancy yet seemed as natural to them as tying their shoe laces, although I wondered how half of them managed to fold their bodies to tie them without muscle getting in the way. Curtis and I kept to ourselves; we said hello and goodbye but the others left a corner of the gym free for us and we just stayed there until Curtis decided we had done enough for the day. He always said it after he touched me. Things were fine while he was standing next to me, checking my posture and telling me what to do. But something always changed when he put his hands on me. I loved it, craved it, but the light switched off as soon as he did it and it was a matter of minutes before the lesson was over. I knew it was because he felt my body change for him. It reacted in a way that was almost entirely new for me and I knew he sensed it. He didn't want me to want him, when he didn't want me back. It was too late; I did want him. Badly. Madly. I was borderline crazy while I waited for every little electric touch.

I felt stronger. I don't know if it was my improved fitness making me physically stronger, or if having something to focus on besides the pain made me a mental warrior. Almost. I was clever enough not to delude myself into thinking Curtis wanted me like I did him. I was fearful enough that he would leave me like everyone else, if I told him the truth. How much I ached for him. How every second of a day spent with him would be my only source of light. I was his dead friend's sister; he wouldn't forget that, so neither would I.

"Do you want to train?" He asked one night as we arrived back at the gym after dinner.

"Can we spar?"

"You want to spar? With me?"

"Sure," I hesitated, waiting for the rejection. I knew he didn't want to touch me. "I mean, the punchbag doesn't duck. And…it could be…fun."

"I don't train anymore, Skye."

"Why not?"

"Sure," he deferred. "Let's spar."

"You're dropping your guard," he pointed out as he tapped my forehead with his gloved hand. "Hands up."

I raised my hands, dropped my elbows and gave him a jab, which he blocked, and then tapped my cheek. He was going easy on me and I still sucked.

"Keep your guard up," he barked, but I saw the enjoyment in his eyes as he got another gentle hit in. "I could go to town on you and take the round with you standing like that."

"This is supposed to be fun," I punched his arm, but I didn't think he felt it.

"It is fun. I can laugh at you," he said. I pouted and stood up straight. "Bend your knees."

"Come on then, Muhammad," I bent my knees. "Show me where I'm open."

"Muhammad?"

"Float like a butterfly, sting like a bee."

"Ah," his laughter made my toes curl and my knees weak. "Come on then, tough girl, in position. I'll show you how you'd get your ass kicked."

The excitement buzzed in my belly with the anticipation. I raised my hands, relaxed my shoulders and breathed out as I looked over the gloves.

"Your defence is off. I can see that without touching you," he tapped one side of my head, then the other, too quickly for me to block.

We stared at each other intensely over our gloves.

"Watch for the body shot."

"What?"

He tapped my head and as I moved to block, he got my stomach. It knocked the wind out of me and as I bent over, he caught me in a headlock.

"See?" He laughed and jabbed me in the ribs. "The ref would pull me back now, but you're done. Exhausted and dazed. Ready to give up."

"I'm not giving up."

I swung my right hand across my body and punched his back by his kidney. He let out a guttural hiss and loosened his grip, so I pulled back and punched his stomach. He bent over and grunted a laugh but as I swung to get his head, he grabbed my waist and reared me back towards the ring and my back hit the canvas. I grinned and stretched out my arms, curling my fingers around the bottom rope as Curtis stepped back. My smiled dropped, replaced by the sudden intense urge to kiss him. His chest was rising and falling with precise, controlled breaths. His gaze matched mine; his eyes glistened and he pulled his gloves off, tossing them carelessly to the floor before holding out his hands for mine. I let him take them off; the only sound in the gym was our erratic breathing and the thud as the gloves hit the floor. I resumed my position on the ropes and sat on the edge of the canvas. My eyes never left Curtis as I watched his eyes flash with barely-contained control, lust and temptation. I wasn't backing down.

He stepped closer and I opened my legs to let him stand between them. He wrapped his hands over mine and leaned closer.

"You want to play dirty?" He whispered in my ear, sending wild heat spreading through my body until it settled as a searing ache between my legs. "I'm the one with the strength."

"Prove it."

He groaned, low at the back of his throat and pulled me off the side. His superhuman legs carried us with ease up to his flat so quickly, there was no time to change my mind, even if I wanted to.

Eleven

Men are confusing creatures. And they think we're the crazy ones…I bought my ticket to Crazy Town…economy, because I was broke.
March 1st, 2003.

Curtis dropped me to my feet as we fell through the final door and separated ourselves from the outside world.

He stopped, just for a second, before his lips crashed to mine and his hands fisted the sides of my t-shirt. He tasted good; like peppermint from the pack of mints he kept in the gym office. The faint smell of sweat from his exertions gave him a virile edge that made me grip the bottom of his shirt and pull frantically. He raised his arms and our lips parted just long enough to get it off. My hands found the smooth planes of his abdomen and as I traced the contours of his body, his mouth moved to my neck and his teeth grazed the sensitive flesh.

I knew his flat like the back of my hand; I gripped the back of his neck and moved us towards the bedroom. I couldn't afford him any time to change his mind. I wanted him like I needed my next breath, which caught in my throat as he took my ear between his teeth.

"Do you want this?" He breathed and a shiver rippled down my spine.

"Yes."

His mouth found mine again and our tongues stroked and caressed. He tore my t-shirt down the middle with ease and it tickled my arms as it fell and pooled at my feet. We kicked our shoes off as we edged closer to the bed and tumbled onto it.

Curtis settled between my legs as I smiled up at him, and he stroked my hair away from my face.

"You're beautiful. You know that?"

"I thought I was cute?"

I shifted beneath him, searching for friction to ease my need.

"You are," his hot mouth traced my neck and travelled between my breasts.

"And adorable," his stubble scraped the lace of my bra as he moved lower.

"And funny," he kissed my stomach and my lips parted.

"And smart," his tongue dipped into my navel and my hips bucked in response as his hands fluidly undone the tie on my gym shorts.

"And sexy," I lifted my hips so he could take them off.

My eyes rolled as he placed a kiss on each of my hip bones. He moved back up my body, leaving a trail of wet kisses and I squirmed beneath him. He swallowed my moan as he took my mouth with his and pulled the lace of my bra down so my breasts could fill his hands.

I felt the desire soak my underwear. Two layers of cotton were all that separated our bodies and I felt him against me as I rolled my hips to meet his hard length. A groan travelled from his mouth to mine. I was a mess of aching need as he sat back and pulled my underwear down my legs, kissed the ball of each foot as he pulled off my socks and his hands slowly travelled higher. I knew I was dripping. I knew he saw it. The look of carnal delight that flashed across his eyes as he looked down at my glistening flesh gave him away.

"Tell me one thing," he rasped, easing a finger inside me and clenching his jaw as I moaned freely and lifted my hips for more. "Tell me you've done this before."

I bit my bottom lip and looked down at his tight body. It was the most tense I'd seen him; proof he was holding back in case I gave him the wrong answer.

"I've done this before."

He collapsed on me. The spring that was coiled tight let loose and his free hand roamed my body, his mouth claiming my nipple and circling, swirling, driving me insane. His finger continued sliding in and out at a torturous pace.

"Condom," he groaned as he moved to the other nipple.

"Cabinet."

It took everything I had to be able to move. I wanted to lie there and take the pleasure until I couldn't take any more. My head was swimming. I couldn't focus on anything but the feel of his tongue teasing me, making my nipples peak and beg for more, and his finger still inside me, making my legs quiver and my stomach tighten.

I found the strength to reach behind me into the drawer and grab a condom. He watched me, his eyes hooded as I tore the packet with my teeth and handed it to him. My stomach flipped with erotic excitement as he lowered his boxers, freeing his straining erection, and rolled the condom onto it. I needed him inside me, buried deep and growling my name.

"Last chance," he took hold of himself and nudged my entrance.

I nodded; I couldn't speak. I lifted my hips and we both let out a silent cry as the first few inches of him penetrated me.

Curtis moved slowly and brushed my hair away from my face as sweat began to collect on my brow. I arched my back as he filled me. It was exquisite; the stretching, the connection, having him on top of me and looking into my eyes as he rolled his hips.

"Curtis-" I whispered.

My eyes closed as my body tightened. Every thrust, every groan that rumbled low in his chest and left through clenched teeth, set my body on fire. I opened my eyes when he plunged in deep, making me cry out. I took in the tension in his jaw, the tightening of his abs and the strength of his arms and finally, I watched where our bodies connected.

I moaned, I sighed, I cried. I gripped his arms and rocked my hips. Curtis drove into me, covering my body with his. All I could do was hold on and absorb every shock of pleasure as he sent it deep into my core. It flowed over me in pulses, each one stronger than the first, building up to something unimaginable.

"Curtis." I begged.

I wanted to let go. I wanted it to last forever. To be consumed and overwhelmed. To be free.

"Let go," he grunted, leaning back and gliding his fingertips down my stomach.

His thumb stroked my clit and I threw my head back. My body shuddered as I cried and gasped; the alien feeling crashed over me and sent me falling. Tears streamed from my eyes as the pleasure moved in and clouded all thoughts, until all I could focus on was

Curtis inside me. I clenched around him and moaned with every wave that washed over me.

Curtis gripped my hips and pulled me onto him. He held me still, buried deep inside me and I felt his cock jerk as he closed his eyes, threw his head back and came with a loud groan.

He peppered my face with kisses as he lay on top of me. We were out of breath, sweaty and spent. My legs were still wrapped around his waist and trembling. It was incredible. I dropped my legs and he eased out of me. He discarded the condom, lay down and pulled me into him. I snuggled into the warmth I had begun to rely on and watched his face as he closed his eyes and let out a deep breath.

"Why did you want to know if I'd done it before?"

I held back the fact that I had only done it once and I wasn't sure if it counted. I had only had sex one time with one person, when I was sixteen, and it was far from the toe-curling, amazing experience I'd just had with him.

"You're a talker," he groaned, but smiled. I loved his smile.

Even in the dark, I imagined how it would have been lighting up his face, temporarily removing the tension he always carried.

"Sorry."

My biggest fear in that moment was that he regretted it. Caught in the moment and not thinking. I was waiting for him to ask me to leave, or to get up and sleep on the sofa like he always did when I stayed.

"I couldn't be your first," he said with his eyes still closed. "Guys like me shouldn't take such a precious gift from girls like you. I'm not one of the good guys, Skye."

"What do you mean, guys like you?"

He shifted restlessly, as if I'd just hit a nerve but I knew, if he could, he would tell me about it. I didn't think he had anyone else to talk to and I wanted to be that person for him.

"I guess there are two ways to look at sex. For the emotion or for the release. Some make it last, take their time, the emotional connection so intense they can't bear the thought of it ending. Others…they look forward to the after, when they're exhausted enough that all thoughts before it are abolished."

I had no idea what to say to that, so after a beat, he continued.

"I'm one of the others. I fuck to forget, not to feel. You shouldn't have sex with guys like me. You deserve so much more than that."

"Is that what that was? You fucked me to forget?"

"Skye-" He opened his eyes but kept his gaze on the ceiling.

"Hey," I interrupted, "I get it. You're my favourite person right now. What just happened won't change that."

Even as I spoke the words, I knew they were lies. I was falling for my dead brother's friend. I knew staying around him would send me spiralling into an abyss of pain I couldn't anticipate. I didn't care. I was prepared for the darkness, even if I only got a few more precious moments with him.

Twelve

It was just me and Curtis. And the hourglass...Damn hourglass.
April 14th, 2003

I fell a little harder for him every day. No matter how much I got from him, I wanted more; maybe because I knew I would never have it all. Every time I saw the Volkswagen pull up outside the tower block, every time he called me on the nights I didn't stay – just to see that I'd gotten home in one piece; every time I looked into his eyes and saw the darkness just beneath the surface, I wanted to help him. I should have backed up, protected my sanity and stayed away, but I couldn't. He was my lifeline and I wanted to be his. I would be there for him, no matter how much I got hurt in the end. I knew how it felt to be imprisoned by thoughts of what could have, *should have* been.

I spent my days with him and he spent them in the office of the gym. He still wouldn't train and I saw the frustration, the tension that sex only temporarily eased. He wanted to train, to abolish the demons and free his mind, but he couldn't. He freed himself with me in the bed upstairs that I had begun to think of as home. Curtis would pull on the gloves and attempt to spar with me, but it never lasted long. We would be tearing at each other's clothes and battling to get upstairs without being seen before either of us had thrown a punch.

I focused on my training to give Curtis space; to give my mind a chance to catch up with my heart. Sometimes I'd watch the guys in the ring, sometimes I tried to practice things I'd seen them doing and sometimes I just pulled on the gloves, closed my eyes and let the punches release my body and mind.

We were emotionally adolescent, Curtis and I. We were both lost and learning slowly together, but I didn't trust him not to leave and, for whatever reason, he wouldn't let me in – all the way in. We spent most days together and fucked every chance we got. He was my friend, my teacher and did things to my body that made me blush for days afterwards.

I couldn't get enough of him against me, but it was a double-edged sword. I wanted to ease his pain and he wanted to ease mine, but I felt like we were running out of time. I was waiting for him to send me away and he was waiting for me to say the L-word. We were both afraid to let go.

Every time we lost ourselves in each other, I fell a little harder for him – for the way he said my name, for his gentle hands as they caressed me and gave me sensual tranquillity…and for the vulnerability in his eyes that was getting harder and harder to hide.

"How's it going?"

I joined him in the office as he clicked away at the computer, and handed him a bottle of water.

"Good," he set his hand over mine before I let go of the bottle and then continued typing. "Are you done training?"

"Mmm hmm," I perched on the edge of the desk next to him. "I think I'm going to go home."

"Why?" He turned his chair to face me and folded his arms.

"It's Friday night. I thought you might want boy time without me cramping your style."

"In other words," he tightened his arms across his chest, "you think I want to go trailing."

"I didn't say that."

"It's written all over your face."

"Then try reading me a bit better. I don't care who you fuck, and you know it."

"Yeah, that's what you *say*."

"Either way I'm going home. Spend the night with a girl, or don't. It doesn't matter to me," he cocked his eyebrow but said nothing. "Why are you being an ass?"

"An ass, huh?" He grabbed my hips and pulled me onto him. "You practically tell me to go and fuck someone else and *I'm* being an ass?"

"I'm not playing games, I'm being serious. I'm giving you the opportunity before I suffocate you and you have to ask for it."

"What makes you think I need the opportunity?"

"You need sex and lots of it."

"I get lots of sex with you," he wiggled his eyebrows and smirked.

"You're such a screw up," I sighed, but couldn't hide my smile.

"Pot. Kettle. Black," he smiled back and I climbed off him.

"Whore."

"Pot. Kettle. Black," he repeated and smacked my butt.

I smacked the side of his head and kissed him on the lips, quickly in case anyone saw – not that I thought about that while I was straddling his lap.

"Seriously, go have fun without me hanging around. You've got my number."

"Mmm, booty call?" He sneaked his hand in the waistband of my gym shorts and the back of his fingers stroked the bare flesh.

"You disgust me," I winked and shoved his hand away.

I heard his roaring laughter as I left the gym and I was sure it echoed around the car park.

Thirteen

Now you see me, now you don't.
April 14th, 2003.

I didn't go home. I went to the park. I didn't care that he would screw another woman; I knew it didn't mean anything to him. It was almost easy to accept because I knew it was a mindless act. I wanted to be the only one who did that for him, but I couldn't be selfish and expect it. I wouldn't let myself be that girl when he made it clear from the get-go that it wasn't what he wanted. I was smarter than to go crazy over something that I had no right to question. I loved Curtis, and for that reason, I would be what he needed and take nothing for myself but what he gave me. I knew what I was getting into. It was my choice.

I found enough change in the bottom of my bag to get the bus back to the tower block. As soon as I stepped onto my floor, I could smell the weed and hear the couple screaming at each other while they smoked it.

"Home sweet home," I muttered to myself as I pulled out my keys.

The door opened before the key slid in the lock and creaked quietly as it revealed the unlit flat. I turned a light on and gasped. It had been ransacked. The cupboards and drawers were open and smoke filled the air. I pulled my phone out to call the police and searched for something smouldering. That's when I saw it. The light on in my mother's room and a cigarette burning on the bedside cabinet. Her room was empty. Her clothes were gone, her bedding was gone. Only her bed, her empty wardrobe and the yellowing pictures on the windowsill of Oliver and I were left. She had gone. I stubbed the cigarette out in the ashtray and shut her door as I headed to my room. My clothes were strewn everywhere and the Adidas shoe box was turned upside down. She had found our savings. All that remained of mine and Oliver's hard work was a five pound note on his bed. She had taken it all.

I fell to my knees and cried.

She had taken everything from me. More importantly, more painful than that, she had stolen from Oliver. It opened a fresh cut, split open the scar tissue and the tears bled from my eyes with every beat of my heart. I couldn't believe she had done it.

I should have hidden the money somewhere else. I should have known she would do it. How could I have been so stupid?

I scrambled to my feet, picked up the money and left the flat. I stood outside as the spring air whipped my hair around my face and called for a cab.

I got fifty pence change from the cab fare to Geoff's and went straight inside. My mind was numb. My head was silent, except for my own voice telling me I had failed again. I let myself into the hallway and up the stairs that led to the flat. I stepped over the threshold before reality hit me. I covered my eyes and stood at the door, listening for Curtis and another woman. I shouldn't have gone to the gym. He was going to think I was crazy.

"What are you doing?"

I heard his voice and a calm washed over me. But the gut-wrenching ache wouldn't dissipate.

"What?" I peered through my fingers, but he was alone. *Thank God.*

"What are you doing?" I heard the humour in his voice, the bastard. He knew exactly what I was doing. "I'm alone."

"I see that," my voice was shaky as I approached him and he turned on the sofa.

He knew.

"What happened? I was about to come and get you."

"You were?" I slumped onto the sofa and fell into his embrace.

"Yeah. The TV is no fun without you attempting to imitate every voice."

"You missed me. You can't deny it."

"To the grave."

That halted the almost light conversation. Grave. Death. Oliver. My mother. I felt my bottom lip tremble. I tried to control it. I tried to hold it in. I couldn't.

The floodgates opened and I cried. I cried for my brother, for my screwed up life of loneliness. I cried for the rejection and I cried because everyone in my life, everyone who was once part of who I was, had left me. And I cried because my ridiculous excuse for a mother stole from the most important person in my life. She threw everything away, halted my plans of getting out, moving on, learning to live without the man who was born mere minutes before me. She had ruined everything.

"Hey," Curtis comforted, but his tightened hold only made me cry harder. "What happened?"

"She left," I sniffed. "She stole our savings and she left."

"Your mother?"

I nodded. I couldn't think of her as a mother. Mothers don't do that. Mothers love their children unconditionally, support them no matter what, and put them first. My mother had never done that and now…Now, I no longer had one.

"What did I do?" The tears continued to fall and I let them. "What did I do to deserve this?"

Curtis stroked my hair and rocked me gently. I couldn't stop the crying. I couldn't make the pain go away. People left, one after the other, but the pain stayed.

I wiped my eyes with the back of my hands and sat up on my knees.

"Make me forget," I met Curtis' gaze and saw the hesitation in his eyes. "Please. Make me forget."

He stared at me and I saw him going over the decision. I couldn't wait. I needed him. For a while, I needed to forget who I was and how I got there. I needed to forget everything I felt, because it was crippling. It was eating me alive. I waited for his answer, and what came took my breath away.

He leaned towards me and I prepared my lips for his, but they touched my cheek; a whisper of a touch that didn't feel real. His kiss took away the lingering moisture from my tears.

"Don't cry," he whispered, pressing his lips to every spot where the tears still laid.

I could feel a new supply building as he took care of me. I'd never been looked after before. I'd never felt intimacy or compassion from another person.

"Give me your pain," he continued to transfer my tears to him. It worked. I felt lighter every time he touched me. "I'll take it away."

Finally his lips met mine, removing the final tear that had settled on my mouth. As his tongue traced the seam where my lips met and I let him in, we shared the pain. We shared the salty taste of my breakdown and he took everything away. He left me with nothing but a fluttering heart and a gentle heat moving through my body. He edged closer as his tongue danced with mine, like the choreographed routine in a ballet; the part where the prince would swoop in and save the damsel in distress, and he laid me back on the sofa. His lips never left mine. Not for a second.

"What would you say if I told you I could give you a new life?"

I was tired, emotionally strung out, physically exhausted and had no urge to move my head from where it lay on Curtis' chest.

"A new life sounds good."

"I can give it to you," he moved so I had to look at him.

"What are you talking about?"

"It isn't really mine, it's Ollie's. I was waiting for the right time and this might be it."

"You're confusing me."

He shifted and rolled over me to climb off the sofa. I watched as he disappeared into the bedroom and re-emerged dressed in boxers and carrying a sports bag.

Oliver's sports bag.

I hadn't even thought of collecting his things after he...

"I knew this would be the last thing you'd think about, so I took it for you," he knelt in front of me and began opening the bag.

"Please don't. I can't," the tears returned as he ignored me and opened up the bag.

"It isn't about moving on. It's just about learning to live with it. You're strong. I know it hurts now, but you're a survivor. You've been doing it your whole life and you can't give up now," I quickly glanced down at the bag, and then back to Curtis.

"Everything Ollie did was for you, including the fight. The stakes were high, he knew he had a shot and he wanted to take it."

"Why?"

"What's in this bag is what will give you a new life," he opened the bag wide and I had to look down. "Thirty thousand pounds."

I stood up and began pulling my clothes on in a panic. There was no way I was accepting that money. I was so angry that Curtis thought I would, I couldn't look at him. I didn't know where I planned to go, but I had to get out. Away from that money.

"Skye, it's what Ollie wanted. If he was here you'd be doing this with him."

"So we're supposed to take my brother's money and run off into the sunset?"

"No," he dropped his head and turned away from me. "It's your money. I'm not coming."

"What?" The blade twisted again, but no tears fell this time. I knew, eventually, it would happen. It always did.

"I can't go with you. Take the money and go. Go and have a career, make friends, do stupid things. Put a deposit down on a flat, or travel for a while. Fall in love. Fall out of love. Fall in love again. But whatever you do, do it for you."

"This is your escape clause," I got it then. Why he'd been keeping the money from me. When he'd had enough or I'd got too close, he had the money to buy his way out.

"No. It's yours. I would have broken your heart anyway. At least, this time, you get to be the one who leaves."

Fourteen

I'm a survivor, I'm gonna make it, I will survive, I'm a survivor. Thank you, Destiny's Child. Thank you.
May, 2004.

I set the final cushion on the sofa and turned it on its point. I looked at my watch. Forty-five minutes. My brand new outfit was set out on my brand new bed, in my brand new room, in my almost new flat. I had forty-five minutes to prepare and didn't know what to do with myself, so I looked aimlessly around my new home, fifty miles from my old one. I had been up all night circling what I wanted from the Ikea magazine; I hopped in my six hundred pound Ford Fiesta as soon as the clock struck nine, and filled it to the brim with good, cheap Swedish furniture. The tin can was bursting at the seams with accessories for the flat, boxes stacked tightly, bags squashed in the gaps and a curtain pole that slid under my headrest so I had to sit millimetres from the steering wheel. I had no hope of seeing in the rear-view mirror. I had lived in the flat for a week and it finally looked how I wanted it. How Oliver and I had discussed. I had taken the pictures of us from my mother's room, given them new frames and they lined the walls in every room in the flat. Oliver was moving in with me, just like we had planned. No would else would be there; I had no friends. I changed my number as soon as I figured out where I was going and only gave my new number to Beth. She hadn't yet called to see where I was living or asked to come and visit. I was alone and I was determined to get used to it. I had already had a year.

I tried not to think of Curtis, but he met me in my dreams. If we weren't on a deserted tropical island holding hands and making love, we were in the gym and Oliver was with us. We laughed and joked and none of the past sixteen months had happened. When I woke up,

I was quickly reminded that reality was exactly that; the painful realisation that, in fact, I had no one.

Half an hour moved quickly and I had to rush to be ready. I caught the bus from my ghetto-like suburb and rode it to the city. I went there often, just to surround myself with people and watch them go about their lives. But today I had a mission. I had read and read and read about the company whose building I was about to step into. Poise. A new, yet established women's magazine. I was the underdog. I had no experience, limited knowledge and nothing to offer; but I had nothing to lose. I had nothing.

"Can I help you?" The man at reception asked with a wide smile plastered on his face. A smile that would make your face ache, no doubt.

"I've got an interview with Nina Bertolli," it took everything not to smile whenever I thought about her name. I wondered if she was related to the olive oil family. "I'm Skye Jones."

"Nice to meet you, Miss Jones," he handed me a journal. "Sign in while I get you a card."

I filled in the details and swapped him the journal for a visitor's badge.

"Eighth floor."

"Thank you."

I looked back as I pushed the button for the lift to see him massaging his cheeks.

"Hi," a little woman with the most flawless mocha skin I'd ever seen greeted me as I stepped out. She was beautiful, with a tiny waist wrapped in a pinstripe pencil skirt.

"Skye Jones," I took her proffered hand and she led me through a bare hallway, stark white with polished black doors. She offered me a seat in the waiting room and a glass of water, but I declined.

"Don't be nervous. It's just a casual chat."

I took a seat then, feeling deflated. I had done my research; Poise already had half a million subscribers. Whether I worked for Nina Bertolli or not would not be decided during a casual chat. They had already written me off. I transported myself back to Geoff's Gym all those months ago and sat up straight. I relaxed my shoulders, took a deep breath and gave my fists a quick clench. I was prepared to fight.

"Miss Jones?" Mocha Lady called from over her computer screen, "Ms Bertolli will see you now."

She pointed to a white door at the end of the corridor. I smoothed my dress down and headed for the office. I wore a red dress because it made a statement; I was there to prove a point.

"Help me, Oliver," I looked up to the spotlights on the ceiling and prayed to my brother before opening the door. No, I didn't knock; she knew I was coming.

"Miss Jones," Nina stood from her chair and held out her hand as I entered the room.

I took it nervously and sat opposite her. She was exactly what I expected, although the bright red hair pouring to her shoulders in soft waves surprised me. I expected her to be blonde. I guessed she was in her forties, with a smile that seemed to reach both ears, accessorised with two rows of perfect pearly whites. There was no doubt in my mind that Ms Bertolli could charm the birds out of a tree.

"How are you?" She asked, her voice chirpy and sweet.

"Good, thank you."

"Great," she pulled out some paperwork and scanned my CV. "So, why Poise?"

"I'm a huge fan of the magazine. I had subscribed before I knew the position was open and I couldn't not go for it. Your company has a great reputation and I'd like to be a part of upholding it."

"But you have no experience in this industry," she popped her glasses on and studied the paper. "Or any industry, really."

Round one to Nina? No.

"I understand that," I replied. "But I have life experience and intuition that means I'd be an integral part of the team."

"Is that so?" She peered over her glasses, but I didn't respond. "I'm looking for someone with experience. A degree, at least. You're not a journalist, your clerical skills are limited and I have a perfectly good working coffee machine."

"It's about what is on the paper?" I wasn't allowing her words to sting. I had no part of me left to hurt. "Someone can be tardy, lazy and rude, but because they've got a certificate in a frame on a wall, that makes them worthy?"

She pursed her lips in an attempt to remain professional, but it looked like a wince. I knew then that I had blown it.

"We'll call you if you qualify for the next stage of recruitment."

She looked down at the papers again and crossed my name off the list.

I stood and moved to the door, but rested my hand on the handle and turned to face her.

"I have nothing to lose. I have no friends, no family, no children. I don't drink, I don't smoke and I'm allergic to cats. I won't be rushing off to feed a feline instead of focussing on my career. And I don't own a passport," I opened the door as she looked up at me in shock. "But what I do have is fight. That's all I have. Determination, guts and loyalty. That's the stuff you can't see by looking at a sheet of paper. That's the stuff that matters."

I left her office with my head held high. I hadn't lost. I was proud of myself.

"Miss Jones?" She called, summoning me like the headmistress. I turned to see almost six feet of her standing at her door. "Do *not* wear the same thing twice in a two week cycle. I don't tolerate chipped nail polish or unwashed hair. I will not stand for hangovers or needing a day off because your boyfriend stubbed his toe. You have one week to prove yourself to me. One week."

She slammed her door and Mocha Lady stared at me, dumbfounded.

"She's been recruiting for months. She must see something special in you, Skye."

"I burn," I smiled with triumph. "Like a skillet."

Fifteen

Oh, Margarita Monday, what have you done to me?
July 26th, 2006.

"Seriously? Michael was hot!"
I poured us another glass of wine and took a huge mouthful. Mocha Lady and I had been friends for two years, although I stopped calling her Mocha Lady when I found out she had a much more exotic name. Penelope Anastas. Her mother, Clarisse, was from the West Indies and her father, Christos, was Greek. It gave her a complexion meant for the camera. She only had to sit by a window for two minutes and she would turn a golden brown. I would have to sit under the sun, soaked in vegetable oil; and even then I'd only turn a painful-looking shade of pink. Penelope was the first person I let into the flat and she had kind of become part of the furniture; we would go back to my place every Monday for a glass of wine before we went out.
"There are lots of hot guys out there. We had a few dates, he was nice, but it wasn't going anywhere."
Michael. I had met him at a charity event a few months back. He was fun, funny in a laugh *at* him kind of way, but he got too close. He wanted to spend every night at my place and asked one too many questions about the pictures on the walls, or why I couldn't go to bed until the dishes had been washed and the cushions arranged in the right way. Clarke was the same. And George…and Steven before that. I met them all the same way; through work. Steven even took me to Paris for the weekend when he had to go on business. Being in the city of love and romance only cemented the fact that I was never going to fall for him. There had been a few before that, too, but I hadn't felt that connection; the one that told me we wouldn't part ways eventually, one way or another. I was content with casually

dating, keeping to myself and keeping an even playing field so I wouldn't feel like I owed anyone anything; enjoying their company until we came to the crossroads where I had to make a choice, to take the risk or protect myself. The decision was never a difficult one. I always protected myself.

"So, you're looking for perfection."

"Nope," I spoke with confidence. "I'm looking for magic. He can have flaws that surpass any list of negatives ever compiled. As long as he's…just…magic."

"You know that crap doesn't exist, right?"

"Yep. Now you see why I do what I do," I clinked my glass with hers. "Come on, drink up or we'll be late."

I didn't know it didn't exist, not really. I *believed* it did. My mother – the pain and confusion halted my breath every time I thought about her – used to care. It was a memory I knew was real. She used to tell me stories; the fairy tales that all little girls believed. Good. Evil. Love. Hate. Salvation.

I had to believe in something when I had nothing and I chose to believe in love. One day I would find someone who loved me as much as the prince loved the princess in every fairy tale ever written. I just had to fight to find it and if I had to date a few frogs, so be it.

Margarita Monday. My favourite day of the week. There was a small Mexican place central to where we all lived and the four of us would go there every Monday. Jose's made the best frozen margaritas.

Penelope and I jumped out of the cab and met the others outside; Jenifer, the new office junior, and Amanda, one of the downstairs receptionists. She would always pop upstairs to gossip and we hit it off straight away. We headed inside and straight to our usual table.

I loved hanging out with the girls. I never thought I would have a group of friends, but there I sat, sipping on a passion fruit margarita and having a good time. I rarely spoke about my personal life and never about the last two years of my teens. I told them I was estranged from my parents, which wasn't a complete lie, it just wasn't my choice to be abandoned. I left that part of my life story out. And anything else prior to 2003. It hurt too much to talk about, so I consciously repressed it, never letting it show.

The lights dimmed and the place fell silent before a new song started.

"*Happy birthday to you, happy birthday to you...*"

I looked around for the lucky birthday celebrator, ignoring the sharp stab in my back, my chest, my heart. I didn't know where it hurt, I just knew that it did. And then my body went numb when I saw two waiters approaching me with a cake and candles bearing the number 24.

"*Happy birthday, dear Skye. Happy birthday to you,*" my friends sang, oblivious to the fact that I had shut down.

The cake was placed in front of me and the tears pooled.

"I'm sorry," I spluttered as I jumped from the table and ran outside.

I hid in the alleyway next to the restaurant and tried to calm myself. I didn't celebrate my birthday. I didn't tell anyone when it was. I avoided conversing about all celebrations; even Cinco de Mayo, and England didn't celebrate it.

"Too much for you, too?"

My head snapped up when the smooth, raspy voice spoke and I gasped when I saw the man it came from. Tall, dark, handsome; broad shoulders, narrow waist, and he was casually leaning on the wall opposite. He had his hands in the pockets of his dark jeans, drawing my attention to his legs – long, strong, powerful. The cotton button-up coaxed my tongue to moisten my suddenly dry lips – a dusting of hair beneath the three undone top buttons, a chest that rose and fell precisely, cooly, confidently.

"It's too hot to eat Mexican in July," he said whilst I continued to mentally undress him. "I damn near choked on my jalapeno."

I looked into his eyes, a dark hazel brown, and laughed coyly. I was spellbound, rendered speechless by the man before me.

"Yeah-"

I was entranced by his five o clock shadow as it darkened with the setting sun, and I was captivated by his eyes when they transfixed on mine and the corner of his mouth turned up into a smile. It was a core-melting smile, a soul-baring gaze; it had me relaxed but on edge. It had me confused. Who was this man?

"You okay?"

I nodded and smiled again. I didn't know what to say. Every man I'd ever met beyond the sleezeballs in bars were at work, where

I played a part. A role. A character. Here in Jose's alleyway, as plain old screwed up Skye, I was tongue-tied, inside out and back to front. He was gorgeous; alluring, self-assured and I was instantly attracted to him.

"Yeah, you just made me jump."

I dropped my gaze and his arms caught my attention as he clenched his fists in his pockets. With the sleeves of his shirt rolled up to his elbows, he looked delicious; I wanted to take hold of them and feel the muscles tense against my palms. There was just something about a man's arms. I wanted to travel up, to feel his biceps that pulled the cotton taut across them, over his chest to the first button and pull. Hard. I wanted to watch the buttons scatter along with my mind. I'd never felt like that before – I'd never felt the urge to possess someone so instantly, and wondered what it would be like to be possessed by them in return.

"Sorry," he smiled when my eyes met his once more. "I can make it up to you."

"You can?"

"Sure. Wanna see a magic trick?"

My eyebrows shot up, my curiosity piqued, "Give it your best shot."

He slowly pushed off the wall and took the two small steps that closed the distance between us. Holding his hand out next to my ear, he snapped his fingers and produced a burnt orange rose. Orange was my favourite colour.

"I'm Thomas."

"Skye," I took the rose from him, lifted it to my nose and inhaled the heavenly scent. "That was some magic trick."

"Skye?"

Thomas and I turned to find Penelope, Jenifer and Amanda at the end of the alleyway. Two men, one blonde, the other with a mop of black curls, stood behind them. All five faces stared towards us, wondering what we were doing. I wondered the same thing.

Thomas cleared his throat and scraped his hand through his hair. I clutched the rose in both hands and stared at the ground. Our friends remained silent for what felt like minutes, but could have only been a few seconds and the awkwardness quickly fell over Jose's alleyway. It was long enough to make me doubt why I'd stayed so long, why I hadn't run away. The girls weren't impressed;

their puzzled expressions betrayed what they were thinking – what was I doing?

"I...uh...I should go," I began to step away. I didn't want to leave, I knew I didn't, but wouldn't admit it.

I turned to face Thomas and held out the rose. He could play the trick on the next girl he met.

"Why don't you keep it and come back inside with me?" He said, his voice vibrating through my ears, warming my blood and making my head light. "I'll renew your margarita."

"I can't," I stuttered, stepping further away. I wanted to stay but I forced myself to leave. "Thank you for the rose, Thomas."

I joined the girls, nodded my heads towards Thomas' friends and took one look back at Thomas. He looked confused but tipped his head goodbye, and I looked at the ground as the girls and I headed towards the cab office.

"Who was that?" Penelope asked.

"I don't know," I shrugged and played with the rose. "I went to get some air and he was just there."

"And you didn't want to stay?"

"No," I whispered, shaking my head. I didn't believe what I said and I knew she wouldn't either.

"Why don't you go back?" She suggested as the others exited the office.

"I can't. He might be dangerous. What if he's a creep?"

I knew, again, my words held no truth. He was just a man and he thought I was just a woman.

"Skye," Jen turned to me and held my shoulders. "What have you got to lose?"

There was that question, the one that put everything into perspective. I had nothing to lose, because I had nothing.

"Go on."

I turned around and followed the girls' gazes. I could see Thomas and his friends further down the road, walking in the opposite direction. Slowly, I took the first step and I didn't look back. I walked as fast as I could, afraid I'd lose him – I didn't know what I would say, only that I would say whatever I felt. I was drawn to him, pulled by an invisible force that brought the panic in. What if

I couldn't catch up? What if he'd changed his mind? Was I about to make a fool of myself?

"Thomas!"

For one moment in time, I didn't care. I ignored the looks from the people around me, I ignored the fear, I ignored the reminders of the past, and I called again.

"Thomas!"

He turned instinctively, as if he felt it too. The pull. He strode towards me as I rushed to get to him and we both slowed to a stop just a metre apart.

"I'm not in the mood for margaritas," I said, taking a deep breath.

"No?" He cocked a brow; a move that had an effect on every one of my senses simultaneously.

It made my heart race, my blood pound in my ears. It made my stomach flutter in excited anticipation.

I shook my head, "Do you like wine?"

He tilted his head from side to side and pursed his lips in thought.

"Red or white?" He shoved his hands in his pockets and rocked back on his heels. "That's the deal maker or breaker."

"Both," I muttered, my confidence failing. He was going to reject me based on whether I liked red or white wine?

"I can work with that," he winked and turned to his friends. "See you tomorrow."

The two men frowned and attempted to protest but Thomas ignored their efforts and held his arm out for me. I hesitated. I wondered if I could do it – go for a drink with a man without a mask in place to protect me. But the question returned; what did I have to lose?

Nothing.

I settled my hand in the crook of his elbow, my fingers flexing against the warm firmness and Thomas led me to a little wine bar on one of the back streets.

We stayed for hours, until the sun had set completely, the cobbled street outside the bar was bathed in darkness and we had consumed two bottles of red wine at the table by the window.

I laughed freely as Thomas recounted things he'd done with Chaz and Joel, the two friends he was with earlier; the places they'd been, the things they'd seen, and now they worked together. We talked a little about me, post-2003, but I kept the conversation on him. I wanted to stay in the bar with him forever; I felt safe, I felt free if only for a while, I felt like I had found something in Thomas and whatever it was, I wanted to keep it.

Eventually, the bar manager asked us to finish up our drinks so they could close for the night; it was past midnight and we'd been there for three hours. I hadn't even noticed. I was happy, content to be surrounded by Thomas and everything he represented. I could be myself around him, whoever that was.

Thomas paid for our wine and we thanked the staff before stepping out into the clammy summer air. Thomas held out his hand for mine and for the first time in a long time I didn't hesitate, I didn't ponder, I didn't shy away. We took the short walk back to the cab office and Thomas ordered a car to take me home.

"Can I see you again?" He asked, tucking my hair behind my ear and setting his hand on the side of my neck.

The goosebumps rose from the warmth of his hand, my pulse thumped furiously against his palm and my body heat rose to match his.

"Yes," I swallowed hard, my voice barely above a whisper.

Thomas blinked slowly, licked his lips and his eyes fell on my mouth. My lips tingled beneath his gaze and the smile that came next was instantly more intoxicating than the wine. He leaned in, so slowly I thought time had stopped. Everything around us ceased to exist as he leaned closer and I closed my eyes.

His lips met mine and Earth stopped spinning. It was a soft kiss, a whisper of a touch as he sealed his mouth over mine. I never wanted it to end, but he pulled away, stroked his thumb over my cheek and as I opened my eyes, his voice, low and assured sent a shiver rippling down my spine as he whispered.

"Your cab is here."

I stepped back and locked into his eyes as he reached behind me to open the door. He had me. I had him. Whatever had happened tonight, I would remember it until I took my last breath. I climbed in the car and as I looked out of the window and waved goodbye, Thomas blew me a kiss. Only it wasn't a kiss; it was his heart, and he took mine with him as I blew one back and the cab pulled away from the curb.

Without warning, Thomas had crept in from out of nowhere and captured me, enraptured me, and given me a reason to fight.

Sixteen

"Wanna see a magic trick?" has got to be the worst way to catch a woman. But it worked on me. Boy, did it work on me. Thomas made falling in love easy.
December 9th, 2008.

"Thomas!" I called up the stairs. "We're going to be late!"
I could hear him rustling around in the bedroom; he took longer to get ready than I did. I humoured myself knowing I'd had all afternoon to prepare for the evening while he was at the office.

Thomas was the managing director for a sports magazine. His father owned the company until he retired and Thomas took over. He was ten years older than me, but you couldn't tell. He acted younger than his age, often blowing raspberries on my neck while I tried to work. He liked to hide too; he'd pretend he wasn't home and jump out of a cupboard when I least expected it. He sat in the same spot for an hour once. And then complained about his knees and back hurting because he'd contorted himself into the little cupboard under the stairs, knowing I'd go there to put my shoes away when I got to his place. Only I was running late.

I acted older then my twenty-five years. I'd experienced things people twice my age hadn't and for that, I was a thirty-five year old in a twenty-five year old body.

I still worked for Poise. I had been there for four years and I loved it. I survived my first week and at the end of it, Nina ripped up my CV and told me I'd never have to write one again. I was an office junior for just eight weeks. I made coffee, ran errands and was at the beck and call of everyone in the office. I moved up quickly and every time I did, I heard the bell ring and imagined the MC announcing that I'd won another round. I had been an admin assistant, a receptionist and I was now the office manager. I loved it;

I had finally found my niche. I felt important, I felt needed. I felt *normal*.

"Thomas!" I called again and heard him laugh.

I moved from the living room to the hallway when I heard him galloping down the stairs. He was tying his tie and trying to wiggle his feet into his shoes, whilst shaking his barely-dry hair into some sort of style.

"Geez, you're a mess," I joked, approaching him.

He continued getting his feet into his shoes while I adjusted his tie and combed my fingers through his auburn hair. I styled it the way I liked it; tussled and slightly to one side. It was guaranteed to have my fingers itching to touch it all night. I liked to tease myself.

"Love you too," he rolled his eyes and squeezed my backside.

"There," I smoothed down his tie and gave him a quick kiss on the lips. I ached for more, but it was all part of our game. My favourite game. "Let's go. The car is outside."

He helped me into my coat, pulled on his dinner jacket and grabbed the umbrella. I took his hand again; a sign of appreciation that he always dismissed, saying he was lucky to have me. I was the lucky one. He understood me; from the moment he handed me the orange rose in Jose's alleyway, he became my magic.

Thomas opened the front door, pulled me into his side until my body melded with his and we laughed with ease as we ran the length of the driveway in the rain, to where the car was waiting to take us to the BBC Sports Personality of the Year awards ceremony.

Seventeen

They say 'don't hate the player, hate the game'. Well, I kinda loved the game...I kinda loved the player, too.
December 10th, 2008.

"That dress makes your tits look incredible."

Thomas curled his arm over my shoulders, taking one of my breasts, sheathed in midnight blue, in his hand.

"Yeah, well, those trousers are too tight. I could see your cock twitching for me all night."

"Mmm," he groaned, moving his arm and slipping both hands into his pockets. "It's been twitching for you for thirty six hours."

That was how long it had been. Sometimes we would only last an hour without each other. Sometimes we'd go at it all night, multiples times, until I was so exhausted I only just made it to work the next day. And sometimes we would go for days with nothing but a teasing touch and a goading glare. It was what we enjoyed most. The anticipation. Building the need until it was on such a base level we couldn't stop for hours. It had been thirty-six since he was last inside me. The only contact we'd had was chaste kissing, an ass grab on his part and a crotch stroke on mine. I ached for him; I would have torn my clothes off and rode him on the back seat if it weren't for the game. We played it every time we went out.

Thomas pulled his closed fists from his pockets and presented them to me.

"If you get it, you go. If you don't, I go," he licked his lips and I knew he had a wicked plan. "Pick a fist."

I thought for a second, just a second, because I was too excited to drag it out, and tapped his right fist. He turned it over and opened it; it was empty. He opened the other. It was empty too.

"Cheating, Mr Radley?"

"We never agreed to play fair," his voice lowered to a seductive, rasping timbre that resonated through me and made my stomach flutter.

He reached for the inside pocket of his jacket and held out his fist again. I pried it open and found a small red gem settled in his palm.

"A ruby?" I took it from him and closed my fingers around its warmth.

"Red. For Christmas."

"Thank you."

He always bought me a gift when we played. I didn't need them, didn't expect them, but I took them. The first time, he gave me pair of Cartier diamond studs. I went crazy and demanded he take them back…

So he wrote the word 'Cartier' on my clit with his tongue again and again, refusing to let me come until I begged for release and promised not to reject his gifts again.

I flushed thinking about that night and squeezed my thighs together.

"You're wet for me already," he breathed and turned to look out the window. "I can smell your sweet nectar. I imagine it trickling from you, waiting for me to lap it up."

I exhaled a moan, just from the sound of his voice and the images of his head between my legs. I'd gone from nought to nymph in seconds. Faster than the flashy car he fucked me on last week.

The car pulled up outside Thomas' house and we climbed out. It sped off into the distance as we waited at the end of the driveway for it to disappear.

"Ready?" Thomas asked, running one finger from the top of my neck to the bottom of my back.

"Ready."

Eighteen

Ready or not, here I come…
December 10th, 2008.

I opened the front door slowly and stepped into the dark house. The anticipation was thick in my veins, slowing my movements so I could savour each second that ticked by on the clock in the hallway. I loved it; the rush, the excitement, the time to imagine every little detail of what was about to happen. I kicked my shoes off one by one, the heels clicking on the wooden floor, and let my coat slide down my arms. I placed it over the banister where Thomas had left his jacket. I closed my eyes.
I listened.
Silence.
I heard nothing but the fast pounding of my heart.
"Thomas?" I called, but I knew he wouldn't answer.
I checked the lounge but he wasn't in there; that would have been too easy. I checked his office next, but all I saw of Thomas was the slideshow screensaver on his desktop. They were pictures of the two of us in The Bahamas in the summer. He'd been in the office to throw me off. It did. I paused and looked at the pictures, remembering the Egyptian cotton sheets that caressed my body along with my lover's hands as the gentle breeze cooled my searing skin.
A bang on the floor above made me jump. I smiled, left the office and ascended the stairs.
"Thomas?" I called again, to let him know I was getting warmer. It was like a radar; the closer I got, the hotter I felt, until it became unbearable. I was trembling with anticipation, burning with desire.
I stopped.

I hooked my thumbs into the straps of my dress and it slid down my body, pooling at my feet like the depths of an ocean. I adjusted my underwear; I knew it would drive him crazy if he was watching me.

I opened the door to the games room and my heart leapt when I saw him. Thomas was still dressed and standing by the window, a dark shadow revealed only by the dim light above the pool table that separated us.

"The games room?" I asked.

I ran my hands down my waist and to the top of my stockings. He made me feel sexy, desirable, and the way his eyes greedily drank me in made me squirm on the spot.

"Come here," he breathed and I walked to him as quickly as my shaky legs would carry me. I stopped in front of him, close enough to inhale his virile scent and I allowed myself to be captivated by the erotic energy he exuded.

"What now?" I rasped, need pouring from my voice.

"Turn around."

I turned away from him and faced the table. I jumped when his strong hands stroked my hair and he gathered it over one shoulder. A simple touch, one so tender, yet it stirred the hedonistic animal within.

Setting his hand on the back of my neck, he gently bent me over the table and I rested my hands on the edge for support as he exposed me to him and his hands found the round globes of my ass. He didn't say anything but I heard his breathing, slow and controlled, as he kneaded my flesh and knelt down. He kissed me just below the waistband of my thong and I moaned as he slid the underwear down my legs.

"I've barely touched you and you're drenched for me," he teased me with his fingertip and held the other hand on my back to keep me from pushing against him.

I didn't tell him I'd been hot for him all night as I tried not to purr in delight every time I caught sight of the subtle bulge in his trousers. I couldn't speak.

"Do you want it?" he asked. "Do you want to feel me deep inside you?"

"Yes."

I threw my head back as he eased his finger in and out.

"Tell me you want it."

"I want it," I begged. "Please."

Thomas spun me around and pushed me into the table. The bottom of my back crashed into the smooth wood.

His fingers tickled the outside of my calf, grabbed the back of my knee and swiftly hooked my leg over his shoulder. I gasped as he opened me up to him and growl of appreciation rumbled deep in his chest as he looked at the glistening flesh between my legs.

"I want you to watch," he said, looking up at me. There was something so powerful about seeing him kneel before me. "Watch me fuck you with my fingers. Watch my face as I make you come. Wait for me to bury my cock inside you and fuck you like the animal you make me."

My core quivered. I was sure he could make me come just from his words, his voice low and hoarse, and laced with lust. I nodded as two fingers slid into me, stretching me; preparing me for his assault.

He started off slow, moving in and out as I watched my arousal coat his fingers. I closed my eyes when his thumb found my clit and all movement stopped until I opened them again and found his gaze. He was watching me. I couldn't look away as he moved faster and I saw the hunger in his eyes. His thumb coaxed my clit to swell as his fingers scissored deep inside me, stroking the sweet spot that set my heart racing, pounding against my ribs. I heard my euphoric cries as my body began to build. I clenched around him as my legs shook and I tried to stay upright. My fingers dug into the edge of the table, but I was lost in his eyes, entranced by his control as I rapidly lost mine. My orgasm crashed into me violently and my release exploded from me.

I fell back against the table and threw my other leg over his shoulder as the spasms wracked my body.

"Thomas," I panted. "Stop."

I tried to wriggle free as the sensitivity clouded the pleasure, but he held me still. His fingers left me, but he replaced them with his mouth. I thrust my hands into his hair and tried to push him away. The intensity had tears streaming from my eyes; I couldn't take any more. I fisted his shirt when he lifted his head and stood up and I pushed him back as I sat.

I wanted more, but I couldn't speak. I continued to shudder, every muscle trembling.

Thomas stepped back and shoved his hands back in his pockets with a dark, triumphant smirk.

I looked at him as my chest heaved and tried to talk, but all that escaped from me were whimpers of desperation as my climax continued to pulse through me.

He knew I wanted him. I could see the triumph as his gaze dropped and his eyes turned to dark pools of onyx. He licked his lips as he looked at mine. I was a mess of liquid heat and wild desire.

He parted his lips and I waited with baited breath for something, anything, to come from the beautiful mouth of the man who often propelled me to ecstasy.

He stepped away.

He changed the rules and upped the ante. Another step back and I climbed from the table and reached for him but he shook his head.

He snagged his bottom lip between his teeth and cocked an eyebrow. His hands lowered to his trousers and he undone them fluidly, allowing his steel cock to spring free.

"Time for the next round."

One hand held his rigid length and the other beckoned me to come closer. I pushed off the table and walked towards him, watching as he slowly stroked himself and coaxed the stream of clear liquid to ooze out. I licked my lips and stopped in front of him, close enough to feel the heat pouring from him. He blinked as his eyes moved to my heaving chest and back to my face. He parted his lips and his warm breath on my mouth drew out a desperate moan. I reached out and began to unbutton his shirt, my fingertips brushing the granite body beneath the cotton.

"I want you, Thomas." I breathed and lowered my hand to replace his.

I curled my fingers around his thick shaft, my free hand slipping into my bra.

"Back up and lie on the table," he said, nudging me backwards and allowing his engorged cock to stand unaided. Stepping back, I watched Thomas undress himself and slid on the table, leaning back on my forearms and waiting. God, I needed him. My arousal was like an inferno and I was quivering with desperation. He approached me slowly.

"Open your legs. Show me how wet you are."

I lifted my feet onto the edge of the table and let my legs fall open. I laid back and closed my eyes, knowing he could see what remained of my last orgasm, and my body's craving for another. I gasped when I felt the tip of his cock touch me, sliding over my clit and teasing the throbbing flesh. I continued to wait, my lust bordering on supernova and ready to explode.

"Please," I begged lifting my hips. "Take me, Thomas. Please."

He slid through my folds, filling me in a second. He paused. I stretched for him, I relaxed, I sighed and I gave myself to him. He moved slowly, easing in and out, teasing me with glimpses of the animal within with surprising thrusts that made my core tremble. He gripped my ankles and held my feet at the bottom of his back. I felt his muscles contracting as he drove into me, his pelvis meeting mine, his loud groans matching my ecstatic cries.

I cried out and mumbled an incoherent expletive when Thomas gripped my hips, arched my back and plunged in deep. I clawed at the felt on the table, but couldn't get a grip. I tried to reach for Thomas but he had me pinned down in position. My core was tightening, I clenched around him and searched for something to grab to control the release and contain the screams. I grabbed two snooker balls and squeezed, breathlessly crying Thomas' name, the slick heat between my legs dripping as I edged nearer to release. The sweat collected on my skin and the pleasure clouded my vision. The sound of flesh on flesh accompanied our moans, his thumb found my clit and the power of his predatory thrusts reached mind-numbing depths. I was close, building without respite and ready to fall.

"Let go, Skye. Come for me. Squeeze my dick and let go."

"Come with me," I panted, holding on, making it last, squeezing tight to take him with me. "Come with me."

He nodded and clenched his jaw, slamming into me until my breasts spilled from my bra and I held them in my hands. The felt against my back began to burn, adding to the sensation that I was on fire.

"Come, Skye!" He growled, squeezing my thighs until I felt the bruising.

I exploded, throwing my head back, screaming until my throat was sore and the quivering reached every nerve. Thomas stilled and gripped me harder. His cock jerked and he let out a roaring cry as he filled me. I felt every pulse deep in my core until he was spent, and slowed to a stop.

∗∗∗

I left the bathroom sore and sated and flopped onto the bed. Thomas covered us with the duvet, tucked me into his side and I ran my fingertips through his chest hair. I pressed a quick tender kiss to his chest, my favourite part of his body because it held the gift I treasured most.

"Sometimes," he said with a sleepy sigh, "I wish I could watch us together. I never know what's on your mind and I get so lost in looking at you, I don't see how you look at me… I saw it downstairs."

"What do you mean?"

"I saw you in the office looking at our pictures."

I tried to move away, but he held me to him. I was suddenly nineteen again and waiting to be rejected for having feelings I shouldn't have had. My mind started racing as I searched for memories of what I'd done wrong.

"Hey," his fingertips traced my neck, over the vein that thumped furiously. "Stop."

"Sorry," I took slow breaths to try and calm down. "Sorry."

"You love me, don't you?"

"I tell you I love you every day."

I heard the aggression in my voice and had to remind myself not to push him away. My instinct was always to push and protect.

"Anyone can say the three words. I love chocolate. I love pizza. I love the lumbar support on the chair in my office. It's different when you mean it. The words become…superfluous."

"So what do I do instead?"

"Let me in," he chewed on his bottom lip. "And kiss me. Kiss me like I'm about to kiss you. I love you too."

Thomas tipped my chin so I looked up at him, gently brushed his lips back and forth over mine and finally, he sealed our mouths together.

"And then," he said, pulling back and stroking my cheek with the backs of his fingers. He eyed me cautiously. "And then move in with me."

I gasped.

"What?"

"Move in with me, Skye."

I panicked.

"I can't."

I tried to back away, but Thomas held me still, shifting and rolling so he was between my legs and I was pinned to the mattress.

"Baby," he chuckled. "I'm not asking you to sell me your soul."

"I know but-"

"Before you explain it," he held his fingertips to my lips and I kissed the pads of his fingers. "I get it. I understand it's a big step, but it isn't irreversible."

"Thomas," I forced a smile through the fear and took his hands in mine. "I'm not worried about that. There's no expiration date on us. It's just- I'm just…weird."

"I know, baby," he patted my head and his stomach shook from holding in the laughter. "I know."

I smacked his hand away and rolled my eyes.

"I'm serious. I'm difficult to live with."

"So am I."

"I'm not a good cook."

"I burn toast."

"I don't like ironing."

"I never put dirty socks in the laundry basket."

He kissed my other cheek.

"I don't like dirty dishes. I have to wash up before bed because I can't get up in the morning to a dirty kitchen."

"I have a dishwasher. It takes seconds to load."

I held onto his wrists as he kissed my forehead and his mouth-watering scent filled my nostrils. I inhaled and released a sigh.

"I like things to have their place. Clutter makes me antsy. Mess makes me grumpy."

"I'm a tidy guy," my turn to give him the look, holding him back as he leaned in to kiss me again. "I'll *be* a tidy guy."

"I don't want you to change. Ever."

"Then what's the matter? You pretty much live here anyway. You stay every night. You've got things here already, you've practically taken over my bathroom."

He tried to be funny, but I could see the worry in his eyes and the nervousness on his furrowed brow.

"It's…Oliver."

I couldn't control the sadness in my voice whenever I spoke about my brother. He was with me every second of every minute of every day. It was why I was the way I was.

"Oliver?"

Thomas sneaked in during my moment of distraction and his lips met mine. His kiss calmed me, relaxed me, allowed me a minute to let the pain fade again.

"Yes, Oliver," I took a deep breath and cleared my throat. "I just want everything to look how he wanted it. I know he isn't coming back but it's all I have to make me feel like I've done something for him. Cushions, dishes, bed sheets. I get anxious when things aren't right and I can't control it."

"Hey," he wiped an escaped tear away and held my gaze. "It's okay. Geez, I love you for it. You don't want me to change, I don't want you to change."

He leaned in and peppered my face with kisses.

"I want you to move in here with me, and bring Oliver with you."

I didn't know if I sobbed or laughed; I was shocked. I was relieved. I was completely and totally in love with Thomas Radley.

"Yes," I whispered, finding his lips through the tears that blurred my vision. "We'll move in with you."

I couldn't tear my mouth from his. I couldn't stop kissing him as I felt the words warm his lips as they left mine. The tears fell and Thomas held me to him as we embraced each other and the step we were about to take.

Nineteen

Deep meaningful conversation, not a fan. Sweet pillow talk, almost a fan. Churros…huge fan.
November 29th, 2009.

I loved our Sundays together. When we weren't in our offices finalising things for Monday, we spent the day in town. It was small and quaint on the outskirts of the city. Wide open spaces, fields of wildflowers, and a trickling stream that ran through the middle of the town, from the old church to the old windmill, made it feel like a world away from the hustle and bustle of the city. A tranquil little spot in the centre of madness. It was our tranquil little spot. I loved being a part of it and had since it became our home a year ago.

We often walked the aisles of the Sunday market. Thomas had a thing for the cheeses and I loved perusing the stalls for fresh eggs and bread. It had snowed in the night and we walked glove-in-glove, wrapped up so only our faces were showing. It had only snowed a couple of inches but, like the stereotypical Brits we were, we had no idea how to react to the alien white fluff besides to wrap up like we were on an arctic voyage and moan about how cold we were.

"I've been thinking."

Thomas pulled me off to the stall selling sweets and looked at the treats on offer.

"Did it hurt?"

"Funny," he looked at me with the puppy eyes I fell for and pouted. He was a terrible actor. "Anyway, I thought we could get a tree this year. A real one, so the house smells like Christmas."

I said the only thing I could think of that wasn't a strangled cry of pain, "What does Christmas smell like?"

"You never had a real tree?" We left candy-free. He knew he'd touched on something I didn't talk about. I couldn't. I didn't even think of those days. Pre-2003. A time that felt so long ago and a world away from the life I now lived. I was back at the crossroads…only this time the decision wasn't easy.

I took a deep breath.

"We had trees. They were just artificial ones with fibre optic lights."

"You had baubles though, right?"

I rolled my eyes, "Yes, we had baubles. And an angel on the top. I had a normal family life until I was eighteen."

"It's okay," we stopped at another food stall. I concentrated on the sweet smell of chestnuts and caramel to distract me from the anxiety that crept in. "You don't have to talk about it. It was just an idea."

I stared into oblivion as Thomas mulled over what the stall was selling. He knew I needed a minute. I wanted Christmas with Thomas, and I wanted to do it our way. The present way, not the past way.

"I don't like chestnuts," I said as Thomas opened his mouth to order some. I turned to the woman running the stall. "He'll have the chestnuts. I'll have a churro with Nutella, please."

"Mmm…Nutella and you?" Thomas wrapped his arms around my waist and whispered in my ear. "Don't lick your lips."

"Cinnamon," I took a bite and offered him my mouth. He kissed me quickly and licked the sugar and cinnamon off his lips. "Cinnamon smells like Christmas."

I remembered making cinnamon biscuits with Grandma before she died. Oliver – I covered my heart with my hand – and I fought over what shape to cut them; he said they all had to be the same shape so they didn't look messy on the tree. I should have let him pick the star, but I argued until he gave in and we cut them into hearts.

We paid the woman and I tucked my hand in Thomas' back pocket; he squashed me to him so he could hold me and eat his chestnuts.

"No tinsel, okay? We'll get a tree but I don't like tinsel, and no moaning because I can't stand the needles on the floor."

"Deal," He kissed the top of my head and I took another bite of my churro. "You're the boss."

"You know it," I bumped my hip into him as we continued browsing the stalls.

I wanted to celebrate Christmas with Thomas. He was the only person I could be free with…besides – no. Thomas was my freedom. My magic. I couldn't go through life miserable and I wouldn't bring Thomas down. His excitement was contagious. I knew why, but it was something else I couldn't allow to cross my mind.

"Here," Thomas handed me a glass of brandy and a slice of the olive bread we bought at the market.

I thanked him and he set my legs over his as he sat down and pulled out a folder. We liked to turn the TV off and relax in the evening, just the two of us like it had always been.

"What are you reading?" I asked.

"Background on some fighters. There's a title conference coming up and we're covering the match. I thought I'd do some research on them."

"Who are they?"

"A guy called Cyclone and Andy Mallone."

"Never heard of them."

"Why would you have?" He squeezed my leg and continued reading.

"Yeah, right." I looked down at my diary and tried to ignore the nauseating nostalgia that made my skin prickle.

"Thomas?"

I knew dropping my voice and massaging the inside of his thigh with my toes would grab his attention. It did. I parted my legs, inviting him closer and he took the opportunity, moving between them and dragging my nightdress up.

It was time to forget.

Twenty

I could do it, I knew I could. I finally believed that I had the gumption to win this battle. I was going to be a champion. November 30th, 2009.

"Skye!"

I jumped when Nina yelled my name from her office; I shot out of my chair and smoothed my dress down as I scurried along the short hallway. I checked my nail polish and touched my hair to feel for grease. I thought I was fine.

"Yes, Nina?" I asked stepping into her office and seeing a stressed Nina pacing the floor. She marched so furiously I was sure she'd leave tracks in the carpet. "Everything okay?"

"No."

She continued pacing, continuously smoothing down her suit jacket, but there wasn't a crease in sight.

I stood with my hands behind my back and waited. Eventually she stepped behind her desk, sighed and sagged in her chair.

"Can you go and get me a coffee?" She mumbled, tossing her glasses onto her keyboard and pinching the bridge of her nose. "And bring your diary back with you."

I nodded and rushed out of the office.

"You okay?" Amanda asked when I fell into the coffee room and began putting together Nina's order.

"Something's up with Nina. I think I've done something wrong."

Amanda winced; we'd seen people after they'd felt her wrath. Most of them left in tears or as white as a ghost.

"I'm sure you'll be fine."

"Yeah, tell me that when I'm out on my ass."

"Good luck."

She gave my shoulder a squeeze as I turned to leave. I struggled to walk fast enough back to my desk without spilling the coffee. I grabbed my diary and as I hurried back to her office, I prayed she wouldn't mind the multiple sticky notes that hung from the pages. Her PA, Erika, had been adding to my to-do list for weeks. Maybe I'd forgotten to do something she'd asked. I shoved it under my arm and opened the door. Nina was massaging the back of her neck and staring at her computer screen when I placed her coffee in front of her and sat down.

"Have you booked flights before?" She asked.

"Yes."

"Meeting rooms? Meetings with clients? Have you spoken with our advertisers? Photographers? Printers?"

"I have before, yes."

She held out her hand for my diary as she inspected her cappuccino and I handed it to her. She flicked through the pages, reading my notes.

"You look organised."

"I am."

When I first got promoted to office manager, Thomas gave me some pointers on prioritising and organising, so I was confident.

"Right," she slammed the diary on the desk and I watched the post-its hang on for dear life. "Here's the deal." She chose that moment to take a sip of coffee. "Erika is leaving. Her boyfriend is relocating to Leeds and she's going with him. You don't have a boyfriend, do you?"

"Yes, I do."

"Ah, yes. Thomas Radley," she purred and swooned in her seat. "That's fine."

Would it not have been fine if it was someone other than Thomas?

"What do you need?" I asked, preparing to step up.

"A PA...I want you."

I didn't see that coming. Through her stress, Nina smiled at my shock.

"Me?"

"Yes, you. Erika can take over the office until she leaves and Penelope will find a replacement. I want you working with me."

"Wow. Thank you."

"Go," she waved me away and turned back to her screen. "Erika will be back shortly and you can swap schedules. She's messy, so you'll have to get a new diary and sort it out. I've got printers running late, next week's cover still not decided and a load of article proofs for you to filter through."

I got up shakily from the chair and headed back to my desk. I was Nina Bertolli's personal assistant. Ring the bell…another round to Skye the Skillet.

"Thomas?"

I dropped my bag on the floor and followed the pheromone trail that told me Thomas was already home. I found him in the kitchen, rummaging in the drawer.

"It's on the sideboard," I said knowing he was looking for the corkscrew.

He turned and smiled at me like he always did – a smile that made my heart beat a little faster.

"Hi, beautiful," he strode towards me and wrapped me in his strong arms. "How was your day?"

"Perfect, actually," I tiptoed and kissed him quickly. "Will you open the wine while I go and shower? I have some news."

"Good news?" He gave me a once-over but seemed satisfied when I nodded confidently.

"Great news," I kissed him again. I just couldn't get enough. "I won't be long."

We sat on the floor by the coffee table sipping our wine after dinner.

"Will you tell me now?"

Thomas had asked all through dinner for the news, but I made him wait. It was still sinking in. It was exactly what I wanted; to be at the top of my profession.

"Mm hm," I took another steadying mouthful of wine. "I got promoted."

"You did?" he didn't seem surprised.

"I did. I am now, well, as of Monday, Nina's PA."

He lunged at me, encasing me in a celebratory hug that sent us back onto the floor. He hooked his leg over both of mine and shifted so he was straddling me. He took my face tenderly in his hands.

"That's my girl," he leaned down and kissed me; slowly, sensually, reverently. "I knew you could do it."

"I'm really excited about it. I didn't see it coming."

"I did," he sat back and grinned down at me. "It'll be tough. I know how hard I work Trisha and I'm a kitten compared to Nina. But you deserve this. I'm proud of you."

I sat up to rest on my forearms as he leaned down and we were nose to nose.

"Thank you."

"Oliver would be proud of you."

We both looked down as Thomas' fingers found my palms and our hands danced together. His hands were warm, always warm, like his heart, and they felt soft against mine as if we were both embracing the magic Oliver had blessed us with. I had no doubt that he brought Thomas and I together. He protected me when I was fragile and now that I was stronger, he was cheering me on. He showed me every day that I was worth something, that everything that had happened hadn't been in vain.

"I love you," I whispered, looking from our entwined hands as they twirled and caressed, to his eyes that sparkled with the pride and love he professed.

"I love you, too," he said. "And guess what?"

"What?"

"I'm taking you shopping this weekend."

"*You're* taking *me* shopping?"

He raised his eyebrows with a smirk, "Yes. Is there a problem with that? My beautiful PA should have a new closet full of clothes to start her new job on Monday."

"Dresses?" He nodded. "Underwear?" He nodded, licking his lips and glancing quickly at my chest. "Heels?"

"Definitely heels," he ran his hands down my legs to my feet and lifted them to lock my ankles on his back. "I'm picking out the heels."

My pulse quickened; I felt it thumping in my neck. I loved it when we had sex with me wearing nothing but a pair of heels. Thomas knew how to make me feel like a woman; safe, desired and loved.

"Deal."

"Deal. I'll just need an extra-large coffee before we begin the ordeal."

I rolled my eyes but before I could think of something smart to say, he lowered his hand and blew a raspberry on my neck. My arms and legs flailed and I shrieked and shrilled as I tried to shove him off me, but eventually, I succumbed to the willpower of the man on top of me and let him have the unrestrained giggled he was the looking for. My laugh was one that sounded like a besotted princess enjoying her beloved prince. I was that besotted princess, totally devoted to my beloved prince.

It wasn't long ago that I was the lonely poor girl, searching for something that didn't want to be found…

Twenty One

Everyone moves on. Sooner or later, everyone forgets. I just wasn't expecting them to disappear altogether.
August, 2003.

Summer was coming to an end. The days were getting shorter and the already torturous nights would just get longer.

I'd done a little travelling like Curtis said. I had been to the Spanish coast and sipped Rioja while watching families enjoying their summer holidays in the sun. I went to the South of France and picked at croissants while I watched couples relaxing on the beach, just enjoying their time together. And I had been to Rome and watched friends enjoying the beautiful surroundings as I savoured gelato. Every place I went to reminded me that I was alone. All of those experiences should have been shared with another; a friend, a family member, a partner. I had none of those things.

I flew back from Italy when I'd had enough and managed to hide in the tower block for a couple of weeks. That was coming to an end, too.

"What are you going to do?" Beth asked when she called.

"I have no idea," I sighed. "The eviction notice was dated while I was away. I have to move out in September."

"Do you want to come and stay with me? Just until you find your feet."

There was a pause. She was offering because she felt like she had to. I didn't like pity; despised it, in fact.

"It's okay. I've got time to sort something out."

"Are you sure? I can send you some money for a train ticket."

"I'm sure. I'll call you when I've found somewhere and we'll arrange a visit."

"Sounds good," I heard a door open and close and the sound of giggling girls wafted through the phone. "I've got to go. Keep me posted. Love you."

She hung up the phone before I could tell her I loved her too.

I couldn't sit in an empty flat twiddling my thumbs, knowing Curtis was just down the road. I tried, I really tried, but I missed him. His presence. I just missed him. I could pretend I wasn't trembling with overwhelming desire when he was near, but I needed him. He needed me too. I convinced myself, while I was away and staring at the four walls of my hotel room, that he did what he did to protect me, because eventually he would break my heart. He couldn't. I had nothing left to break.

The taxi pulled up outside Geoff's Gym and I climbed out. I knew straight away that something was wrong. The energy, the pull that drew me in to the building in a car park, was gone.

"Excuse me?" I called to the man with his back to me, locking the door.

"Can I 'elp you, love?"

He turned to face me. It was Geoff. I had seen his pictures on the walls in the office with some of the great names in mixed martial arts. Curtis was right; he did have a weird cockney accent.

"You're closed?"

"We are," he dropped his gaze to his worn Timberland boots and I watched him force a recovery.

"When are you back open?"

"We won't be op'nin' again," I saw the sadness in his eyes and the defeat in his sallow skin. "What d'ya need?"

"Uh-" I searched for something, anything. "A friend of mine wants to start training...Why are you closing?"

I pulled my denim jacket tight around me as I watched his eyes glass over.

"We were a team," he stared off into the distance and started walking. I walked next to him and kept my eyes on his ashen face. "It's like the foundation of me gym. When one falls, everything falls. We lost one of our boys in January. We tried to carry on, but the magic was gone. We can't carry on without 'im, so we're shutting down."

I stopped walking. I froze. They stopped training for Oliver. All of them. But I'd watched them train; I'd seen the magic, Oliver's magic. In all of them. I didn't understand; I thought it fuelled their passion.

"Y'alright, love?" I nodded as my mind raced with confusion. "What d'ya say ya name was?"

"Pamela," *I lied, forcing myself to function.* "I'm sorry about your fighter. Good luck."

I nodded my goodbye and headed in the opposite direction.

"Pamela?" *I turned around, thinking I'd been caught.* "Tell ya mate there's a couple gyms just outside town."

"Thanks."

I walked away, void of emotion, but almost satisfied that I had punished myself a little more by using my mother's name.

Twenty Two

I hated the thought of not being home. I hated the thought of returning back, to find him gone. And I hated the thought that he would get in after work and wonder if I'd be out...again.
December 18th, 2009.

"Nina," I sighed, "I've been putting this off for weeks."

I was in one of my panics after being summoned to Nina's office. I knew why and I was dreading it. My professional life was planned to the minute; I was the epitome of organisation and control. My personal life, not so much. It was a disaster and it was my job's fault. Thomas and I had been trying to go Christmas shopping for weeks, but I cancelled time and time again. I blamed the fact that while he was the boss, I *had* a boss, but it was gradually losing its validity.

"What's another night, then?" Nina wiggled her eyebrows in a silent challenge and the wicked look in her eyes got me.

"Last time. Seriously, last time."

"Blah, blah, blah," she waved her hand, dismissing me.

I sighed. I had to learn to say no; it was both my greatest asset and biggest flaw. I really did just want to go home. I wanted to eat dinner with Thomas, finish the wine in front of the fire listening to Keane and climb into bed.

He wouldn't be surprised to find me not home.

"Come on, sour puss," Penelope called between our cubicles. I sat down, furiously rubbing my temples. I had a stress headache.

"You know why she's doing this, don't you?"

"Of course...Am I complaining? No."

I shook my head and logged out of my computer.

Nina's husband had just left her. I had no idea she was married, until she sent me to collect the divorce papers. She had just become a divorcee, at fifty-two. Days before Christmas.

She was married to her job, not to the man who waited up for her most nights to find she'd fallen asleep at the office.

As we left the offices of Poise, I thought about the man waiting for me. I checked my watch. He would be just getting home. He would call my name from the bottom of the stairs, thinking I'd be in the bedroom getting changed. But he wouldn't get an answer. I was on my way out, again, so Nina didn't feel alone. I felt sorry for her, but I couldn't help wondering why she could go for dinner with us, but couldn't go with her husband when she had one.

Thomas and I both had hectic jobs, but we worked because we both fought for it. I was working seventy-hour weeks over the Christmas period as Poise funnelled winter fashion advice, gift ideas and celebrity gossip into the greedy hands of the female population, and Thomas was busier than ever as titles in every sport were being played for. Our quality time together had gone from dinners at our favourite restaurant and nights in front of the fire, to reaching for the same slice of toast as it popped up and feeling lucky if we brushed our teeth at the same time in the morning.

I hadn't made it to bed before he fell asleep once in the last seven days and I missed him.

Nina's driver, Darren, hopped out of the car and gave us a cheeky smirk as he opened the door and we filed into the back.

"Ssh!" I tumbled in the front door and fell to my hands and knees.

It was easier to stay like that, so I crawled along the hallway and flopped onto the bottom step.

"Thomas!" I called, then covered my mouth. "Ssh."

I giggled as an upside down Thomas appeared at the top of the stairs and made his way down. He'd been awake waiting for me, probably reading in bed, judging by the boxers hanging low on his hips and the glasses that framed his hazel brown eyes.

"Long day at the office?" I rolled my eyes at his sarcasm.

"You know I don't want to go."

He snorted, "You could stick to lemonade."

He picked me up and carried me upstairs to our bathroom.

"You've met Nina," I shoved my toothbrush in my mouth.

"I have," he pulled my hair from the tie and I shivered as his fingers combed through my dark locks. "I think she's tameable."

"You can tell her that on New Year's Eve."

Our eyes connected in the mirror. I wanted him; in a split second my blood turned to molten lava. He winked - a sign that he knew exactly what I wanted... I knew he wouldn't give it to me when he turned and left the room.

I pulled everything but my silver thong off and left my clothes on the floor as I stepped into the bedroom. Thomas cleared his throat when he looked up and his eyes followed me around to my side of the bed. I climbed in without looking at him and faced the other direction. Two could play the teasing game.

Thomas pulled me into him and I felt the hard bulge in his boxers against me. I hummed and wiggled into him, but neither of us were going to give in.

"I get you back after Christmas, right?"

I clenched my jaw, wondering how he kept his cool when I was ready to jump him. A moan escaped without permission when he rolled his hips and squeezed my leg.

"Right."

He kissed my shoulder, sinking his teeth in for just long enough to drive me crazy. We closed our eyes and fell asleep with a gentle, smouldering desire swimming through our veins.

Twenty Three

We wish you a merry Christmas, we wish you a merry Christmas, we wish you a merry Christmas and hope it's not as gut-wrenching as the last.
Christmas Day, 2009.

I opened my eyes as the winter sun streamed through the windows. My heart grew heavy as soon as I remembered what day it was. Christmas Day. I groaned and turned to find Thomas; he was on his side, awake and watching me.

"Merry Christmas," I said with as much enthusiasm as I could and kissed him. "How long have you been awake?"

He shrugged, "I like to watch you sleep. You were dreaming."

"I was?"

"You said you missed him."

It hurt as much as the first day. I hadn't moved on from Oliver's death; I had just learned to live without him. The pain never went away. I still struggled to talk about it.

"Do you want your gifts?" I sat up and reached into the bedside cabinet for Thomas' stocking.

"I'm sorry," he smiled weakly as we swapped gifts. "I just want you to have a good day. I know it's going to be hard."

"It will. But I'm spending the day with you. It can't be anything but perfect."

We piled the gift bags into the back of Thomas' car and climbed in. It was tradition in the Radley household to spend Christmas together, and I was a part of that.

We pulled up outside his parents' house and struggled with the bags up the long path to the front door. Thomas' mother, Francesca, opened the door and I felt underdressed in my jeans and knitted jumper when I saw she was dressed for dinner. Thomas shook his head in exasperation, but kissed her warmly on the cheek. He had dressed casually, too, in jeans and the cream jumper I bought him for Christmas. The cream made his eyes the colour of strong coffee and I had spent most of the morning lost in them as he talked animatedly.

"Merry Christmas," she sang. She was a Christmas person. "Everyone is here already. You missed the Buck's Fizz." She paused and looked back at us, "Wow, you two look good together."

Before we could respond, Thomas' legs were trapped by limbs of children. His two nephews, Tommy and Jake. They were his sister, Ava, and her husband's children and they soon followed to greet us with Martin, Thomas' father.

"Uncle Tom!" The boys cried, tugging on his jeans and covering the denim in snot and melted chocolate.

"If you don't get off, you won't get your gifts," he laughed as they dropped to the floor and looked up at him, grinning.

"They're great boys," I said to Ava as we helped Fran clean up after dinner.

"Thank you, we got lucky," she laughed. "You better hope the well behaved gene is in the Radley DNA."

I chuckled uncomfortably and agreed, and scrubbed harder with the drying cloth. Kids weren't going to happen. It wasn't that I hadn't thought about it, I had. I got broody like every other woman and I had maternal instincts, I knew I did. Those instincts were just overshadowed by my past and replaced with the fear of failing like my mother did. I was scarred. I wouldn't have children because, like my mother, I didn't deserve them. I pushed the thoughts aside and watched Thomas, marvelling at his excitement as he helped the boys open their gifts. Tommy and Jake were the reason he was so excited about Christmas.

Ava and Kevin lived in Jersey and the only way we would see them would be to holiday there, and we hadn't yet. He was good with kids, naturally paternal, which no doubt came from him being a bit of a goofball, and he spent the day playing with the Scalextric we bought the boys.

He had a great family; relaxed and happy around each other. Francesca and Martin were affectionate, the kind of behaviour I was afraid of before I met Thomas. I had happy memories of my family, each one vague and clouded, and I couldn't be sure if they were real or just what I wanted to believe.

"It's getting late."

Thomas stood from the sofa and held his hand out for me. I was tired, emotionally exhausted from having to pretend I wasn't dying inside, wishing Oliver was here to celebrate with us. Tommy and Jake were in bed in Thomas' old room and we had been snuggled on the sofa talking.

"Will you be here for New Year?" Fran asked as everyone stood and we made our way to the front door.

"We've got a company celebration," Thomas said. "I've got to go and show Skye's boss who the *real* boss is."

I smacked the top of his arm and turned to his parents.

"Thank you for having me over today."

"Nonsense," Martin waved his hand in dismissal, much like Thomas had a habit of doing when he deemed thanks unnecessary. "You're part of the family now."

My chest tightened and my eyes blurred until Ava pulled me in for a hug. I had a chance to rein in the emotion with my head in the crook of her neck before she freed me.

"Anyone who puts up with Thomas is family in our books. Let's get together."

"Definitely," as long as she didn't bring up kids again.

We said our goodbyes and Thomas held my hand as he led me to the car.

"That's another year you've survived a Radley Christmas." He said as he pulled away from the house.

"I love your family."

"I'm just sorry yours aren't around to see how amazing you are."

"Thomas-"

"I know. We don't talk about it. Just know that you can, if you need to. I'm not going anywhere."

"Thank you."

There was a long silence as I watched the streets go by from the window of the car.

"I miss them all," I spoke quietly, unsure if I really wanted to say it. "I never understood what happened. One minute we were happy and the next, it all fell apart. I miss Oliver the most. He didn't choose to leave me, he was taken. I'm not the same Skye I was back then and that's why I don't talk about it. I repressed it so I could survive."

"I would love any form of you. I would have fallen for you no matter what," he pulled my hand onto his lap, but I kept my eyes on the world outside. "Is that what you do now? Survive?"

"It's what I did for a long time. It wasn't about living, it was about surviving. It was about making it through each day. How could I live, when Oliver couldn't?"

"Have you ever thought about living for both of you?"

I turned to him and leaned over to kiss his cheek.

"I do live. With you. I never thought I'd have that."

"You'll always have it."

I nodded. For once, I didn't feel like eventually, he would leave me too.

Twenty Four

Should auld acquaintance be forgot and never brought to mind...Damn auld Lang Syne.
New Year's Eve, 2009.

"I love your curves."

Thomas made me jump as I arranged the cushions on the sofa and I turned to see him leaning against the doorframe, watching me. He was dressed for the party and biting his bottom lip. He looked utterly fuckable and charming; his usual self, and I loved it.

"Thank you," I turned slowly to give him a show. "Are you ready?"

"I am. Come here."

I stepped into his arms and accepted the kiss that made his lips the same deep red as my lipstick. I wiped it away with my thumb.

"No game tonight," I said, keeping my eyes on his mouth. I slid my hand down and cupped him through his trousers. He hardened instantly. "I want to know that I can have you whenever, however, wherever."

"As you wish," he covered my hand with his and we stroked him together. "The car is outside."

I dropped to my knees and took our hands away; my teeth grazed the outline of his hard cock, constricted in his trousers. He hummed and I heard him swallow.

"No rules tonight," I stood up, tapped his chest and left the room.

"Nina."

Thomas and I approached my boss, surrounded by her guests. Thomas held his hand at the bottom of my back and I caressed my champagne flute. It was our usual position; it showed other women he was taken and it showed other men I wasn't interested. It showed neither of us were available for conversation that wasn't professional. We didn't want anyone bursting our bubble without permission.

"Here she is!" Nina pulled me away and squashed me to her. "Beautiful dress. I told you Bruno was the man for you."

"You know what you're talking about," Nina had recommended Bruno to me and he gave me a black cocktail dress. It was simple and classy. "You've met Thomas."

I stepped back to him, but Nina smothered him before we could resume our position.

"I have," she held him at arm's length. "Mr Radley, you get better looking every time I see you."

"No one's looking at me, Nina. Your beauty lights up the room," he kissed her hand, then her cheek and I shook my head, smiling. Charmer. "A great party as always."

Nina winked. She knew she'd rocked it; she always did. She threw the biggest New Year's Eve party every year; the best money could buy. Champagne, h'ordeuvres, live music, chandeliers, a mixologist and a bar that sparkled black and gold. All set out in the grand estate that was The Bertolli Household. Even when she was married, the estate was named after her. Nina and Thomas could no doubt charm the pants off each other all night. I was still socially awkward; I had never been able to play the charm game with Thomas. He simply ensnared me and I never wanted him to let me go. But it was time to take him back from my boss.

"Come on," I took his hand. "Nina, you're in demand, and I owe my boyfriend a dance."

Nina purred playfully and clawed at Thomas' arm as I pulled him away and to the dancefloor.

"I'm not sure who won the bet," Thomas said taking me into his arms. "She's quite…rabid."

I gave him the 'I told you so' look and settled into his embrace. We fitted together like a jigsaw puzzle, his 6'1 a perfect match for my 5'7 and he settled his hand on the bottom of my back as we laced our hands together on his chest.

"We get to start another year together," he said, pressing his lips to the top of my head.

"We'll end another one together, too."

He sighed with relief and we danced in silence as the rest of the party disappeared. I hated that he did that, waited for me to leave him. I knew it was my fault because I was waiting for him to do the same. I looked different on the outside; I had money, a career and the life many strive for. But I was still the same girl from the turn of the century, lost and frightened. Only I wasn't alone anymore. I had Thomas and I had to show him how important he was.

The guests gathered in the centre of the hall as the countdown began. Everyone counted, waiting for the new year to arrive, but I turned to face Thomas. I looked into his eyes as he counted down to the beginning of our next year together. His eyes shone, his smile made him appear younger and his hands held mine like he didn't want to let go. It was always like that when I looked at him. It felt like magic, every time. The clock struck midnight and the cheers erupted, but I didn't cheer. I didn't celebrate. I reached up and kissed Thomas. I tried to show him, without saying the words, that I loved him and I was in it for life.

I stepped back and opened my eyes, but I didn't look at Thomas. A familiar face was just behind him, stood still in the middle of the celebrating crowd. His face no doubt matched mine. Confusion. Shock. Pain.

"Skye?" Thomas called.

I looked up at him, remembering where I was, but when I returned my gaze, the face was gone.

"One minute," I squeezed his hand and took off, running through the party as I looked for him. I didn't know where to go; I simply let my feet guide me.

I stopped outside the house, but I was alone. I saw nothing. No evidence from the past that had reared its ugly head to remind me how much I hurt. I scanned the front yard and called out, again and again.

"Curtis!"

Twenty Five

I wasn't stalking. You couldn't stalk someone you couldn't find. You couldn't stalk a ghost.
October, 2003.

The Ford Fiesta was good. I expected a shit wagon when I only paid six hundred pounds for it, but Berta – yes, I named her – and I were good friends. Companions. Lone rangers on the endless roads we travelled together.
I pulled up in a parking space and killed the engine. I checked the name of the place against the leaflet in my hand and I climbed out of the car when I had confirmed I was in the right place.
I was nervous. I always got nervous before the next part. I was hopeful, but prepared for disappointment. If I didn't have hope, I would have given up a long time ago.
I walked towards the building and swung open the door. It smelled of sweat and I heard the rhythmic pounding I had come to rely on hearing to keep me motivated.
"Hi," *I croaked to the nearest beef cake.* "I'm looking for someone, can you help me?"
"Sure. What does a little thing like you want with someone in here?"
Asshole.
"I'm looking for a fighter called Cut Throat. Does he train here?"
"I don't think so," *he waved to one of the two men in the ring.* "TJ?! Anyone called Cut Throat here?"
TJ looked around and shook his head. The other guy turned back to me.
"You're out of luck. Anything I can help you with, sweetheart?"

"No thanks," I stopped at the door before leaving. *"Your stance is shit. Float like a butterfly, asshole."*

I didn't bother looking back. I headed straight to the car and picked up the next flyer, adding the last one to the rapidly growing pile on the back seat.

Where are you, Curtis?

Twenty Six

Some people have sex to forget. Some to remember. Some to feel.... I wanted it all.
New Year's Day, sometime after midnight, 2010.

I was out of breath when I walked back into the house. I had called Curtis' name until my throat was sore, but he wasn't there. I didn't know why I wanted to find him, I just felt like I had to. I should have been angry - he disappeared; he left me like everyone else. I spent months looking for him to find nothing. I scoured every boxing and MMA gym I could find, but he was gone. He just disappeared from the circuit without as much as "I'm still alive". I got angrier with every step I took. He was there, he saw me, and he ran away after making sure I saw him. I was so angry I clenched my fists until they shook. I wanted to find him, just to punch him; to get the satisfaction of making him feel even a tiny bit of the pain he'd made me feel.

"Skye," I walked straight into Thomas. In my erratic state, I didn't see him. "What happened?"

"Nothing."

"Don't lie to me," he took hold of my elbow and steered me back outside. "What happened?"

I paced the front porch, trying to calm myself down.

"Remember what I said about my past? About how I'm different now?" He nodded, "Well, I lived fifty miles away from here and someone from my old town just turned up… It made me forget who I am for a minute."

He opened his mouth to talk, but I held my finger to his lips.

"If you want to talk, we'll talk. But right now-" I shimmied out of my underwear and tucked it in his jacket pocket, "-find us the nearest surface."

He gave me the look; the one that questioned my motives. I gave my own look back; one that told him I wanted him, and I smoothed his jacket down.

"I told you. Whenever, however, wherever."

I tugged his lapels and pulled him towards me, crashing my lips to his and tasting the brandy on his tongue as mine sneaked out to explore.

Thomas slid his hands up my thighs until my dress revealed the naked flesh beneath and he lifted me up to wrap my legs around him.

"Where do you want it?"

"You could fuck me against the window for all the party to see and I wouldn't care. I just want you."

"Hmm…" he nibbled my ear as he thought about his options and his tongue dipped inside before he spoke. "Hold on tight."

He carried me across the lawn, the tightness in his trousers brushing against me. I didn't care where we were going; I kissed his neck, sucking and biting, smiling when his step faltered and he groaned.

"Thomas!" I shrieked when he sat me on something cold.

"Ssh," he covered my mouth with his hand, then his lips and pulled back.

I looked around me. I was on the bonnet of Nina's car.

"Thomas."

He squeezed my legs, his thumbs stroking so close to where I ached for him.

"She'll never know. It was this or lying you on the lawn," his thumb reached the sweet heat between my legs. My body convulsed, begging for more. "Besides – you'll never be able to get in this car again without thinking of me fucking you in it."

"In it?"

He nodded, dropped his hands and walked round to the passenger side of the car. I followed as he opened the door and climbed in.

"How did you know it would be open?"

"Lucky guess."

My eyes widened when he tapped his lap and I almost combusted on the spot when he undid his trousers and tugged them down. No underwear. An engorged cock straining under its weight. And then his voice; low, hoarse, seductive.

"You're not the only one who wants it anywhere, anytime, anyhow. Come here."

I hitched up my dress, climbed over him, setting my knees either side of his legs and lowered myself onto him. A loud cry escaped us both as Thomas impaled me and every glorious inch lead me closer to home.

Twenty Seven

I could tell him everything, right? I could let him in and not worry that he'd be disgusted by my very existence and cast me out onto the streets like an unwanted dog after Christmas, couldn't I? I wasn't so sure, but what choice did I have?
New Year's Day, 2010.

Thomas was still asleep when I woke up and I laid and watched him for a while. He was my everything. I found him at a time when I had nothing and I would forever be grateful for that. He'd had a great life and far more experience than me; blame the age, or whatever, but it was me he wanted. He had a career, a good one borne of real hard work. He had a degree in journalism and another in business management. He had worked his ass off as a journalist for Martin so he earned the right to take over. He had travelled, to Europe, to the Middle East and America. He had sampled the cultures in countries on every continent and he had done it all before turning forty. But it was me, boring, broken Skye with no degree, no heritage, no family and nothing to bring to the table that he wanted. It was me who he chose to share his life with. He was all I had and I didn't need anything else.

I watched him stir as he woke up and caressed his cheek until he opened his eyes and they focussed on me. Last night was amazing. We fucked in Nina's car and then got a cab home and made love in our queen-sized bed.

But we hadn't talked about what happened and I owed him answers. I knew everything about him and it was time to give something back.

"Morning," he smiled and kissed my lips.

"Do you still want to talk?"

I was terrified. If I told him, I risked losing him. If I didn't, I would lose him. I was at the crossroads again, but neither direction looked good. I had to expose myself, let my guard down and become vulnerable to his rejection.

My instinct was to distract us with sex, as I watched him guzzle his water from the glass next to the bed, but I had to control myself regardless of how much I wanted him and how desperately I wanted to avoid this conversation.

"Skye, it's okay to keep things to yourself. Some things. Not things that affected you like last night."

"I don't want to keep things from you. I'm afraid. I was poor, hungry and alone. Years ago, I wouldn't have deserved everything you have given me."

"You're not alone anymore. And I would have loved you then. I don't love you because you're not poor and can eat more than me."

I laughed. I *could* eat more than him. I could eat a double cheeseburger and fries until my belly doubled in size and still have room for dessert.

"The worst part, after losing Oliver, was trusting someone again. Curtis had been through as much as me and I thought we were there for each other. He was there the night Oliver died. He stayed with me in the hospital and never left. We spent every day together until he sent me away. I guess I should have seen it. We were both too broken to fix each other."

"What happened?"

"He kept Oliver's money and gave it to me the night my mother stole everything. He told me to go and live. I thought he was coming with me, but that was never his plan. I travelled a bit, but I was lonely and I missed him. When I came back to find him, he was gone. He just disappeared. I tried to look for him but I never saw him again. Until last night."

"He was at the party?"

I nodded, "Maybe he wasn't really there. Maybe I was looking at a ghost."

"Did you love him?" I shrugged. "Come on, we've talked about Sarah."

Sarah. His crazy ex. When they broke up – her decision – she covered the front of his house with eggs and flour, defaced his football trophies with a butter knife and stole his graduation caps.

"I thought I did. He was Oliver's closest friend and he became my only friend. I don't know what would have happened if he didn't leave, but in a twist of fate, I found you. I wouldn't change that for anything."

"Do you want to try and find him? I have people that can try and track him down."

"You'd do that?"

He nodded and met my eyes with honest sincerity in his, "Without a second thought."

"Thank you, but no," I said as I locked our fingers together. "If I did see him last night, he knows how to find me. I'm not chasing a ghost. I just want to focus on our life together. I'm not that girl anymore."

"I'm sorry he hurt you."

"Me too…but it gave me you. That's worth every bit of pain I've ever felt."

"In that case," he threw the duvet back, exposing our naked bodies. "You can make breakfast."

Twenty Eight

He was a caveman, my caveman, and my God did he look good standing at the barbecue.
August, 2010.

"He's definitely the best looking so far," Penelope nudged me and reached for her glass of Margarita a la Thomas. He was a bartender when he was at university and liked to spoil us girls with his skills.

"You've been saying that for years."

"Because it's true."

The four of us - Penelope, Jenifer, Amanda and I were lounging in the garden. Thomas, Chaz and Joel were at the barbecue arguing over how long it took to cook a steak rare.

"Listen. My barbecue, my rules. If you don't like it, host your own."

He picked up his beer and looked at me as he brought the bottle to his lips.

God, he was delicious. He had marinated the jerk chicken overnight and the smell filled the garden. My mouth watered, but it wasn't the chicken that had me salivating; I wanted to devour the chef. His body was an intoxicating statue of god-like proportion, only made sexier by what was beneath the muscle. He was everything I wanted; there wasn't anything I didn't love about the man standing over the barbecue.

Jenifer whistled and all three turned around and shook their derrieres. We erupted into fits of laughter and the boys resumed their argument, this time over whether burger buns should be buttered.

"This is the life, huh?" Amanda said draining the last of her cocktail and shaking her glass at Thomas for another.

We all hummed in agreement and raised our faces to the sun.

"Now all you need is a little thing in a nappy running around clutching a blankie."

Time to change the subject. I dropped my voice so only the girls could hear.

"I want to plan a party for Thomas. It's his birthday next month and I want to do something special."

They all sat up and crowded around me. The shrieks of excitement told me they'd forgotten about baby talk, thank God.

Twenty Nine

Balloons, check. Banners, check. Mini sausage rolls, check...shock to the system, check.
September 24th, 2010.

Turns out, I was good at being sneaky. I was good at conspiring. The girls and I had spent the last month planning Thomas' party and Nina gave me the Friday off work to get everything ready. I could have booked a venue, but I planned to have a party at home, where Thomas could relax and celebrate with his family and friends. Penelope and I decorated the house with as many fairy lights as we could without it looking tacky. Jenifer collected the bouquets of black and gold helium balloons and Thomas' gift. Amanda, at 5'10 and taller than the rest of us, hung the banner I'd had printed above the entrance to the living room.

I put the CD in the sound system and turned it on so Thomas' favourite music played in every room downstairs. Together, the four of us moved the furniture to open up the lounge and I sat Oliver's picture on the mantelpiece. He would be at the party too.

I left the others to put the finishing touches to downstairs while I headed upstairs to change. Thomas called as I pulled my dress from the wardrobe.

"Hello, Birthday Boy."

"Remind me to stay away from the office on my next birthday."

"That bad, huh?"

I smiled to myself. I had asked his PA, Trisha, to leave all his correspondence until the last minute to keep him in the office late.

"I'm the only one here."

"Oh, are you?" I heard the edge in his voice and responded willingly. "What are you doing?"

"Scrolling through some files. I should be reading them, but I'd rather be at home with you."

"You can pretend," I sat on the edge of the bed. "Imagine I'm there, sitting on your desk and leaning in. I'm so close you can smell my perfume. Imagine I sit forward and stroke your leg. My hand is moving higher."

I heard him shift in his chair and his breathing became uneven.

"Mmm," he groaned. "Tell me more…I'm getting hard for you."

"I know. I can feel it." I could. The tense, erotic energy travelled through the phone and I squeezed my thighs together. "Undo your trousers."

I heard the unbuckling of his belt and the harsh sound of his zip.

"Take hold of yourself and imagine it's me…stroke slowly like I would. Run your thumb over the tip. Catch the pre-cum that oozes out and know I want to taste it, to spread it down your shaft with my tongue."

He sighed and groaned, and his chair creaked as I imagined him tensing his legs as the pleasure took over.

"So good. The way you squeeze my dick makes me crazy."

"Good. Squeeze harder, pump faster. My other hand is moving between my legs. I'm so wet for you. So hot."

I parted my lips and circled my clit with the tip of my finger. I almost couldn't speak through the ecstasy that quickly built. Thomas grunted through the phone, his breathing ragged as he worked himself. I moaned and dipped a finger inside me, spreading the wetness over my swollen nub.

"I'm close, Thomas. My pussy is squeezing my finger like my hand is squeezing your cock. I want to tighten around you while you fuck me on your desk…Tell me you're close."

"I'm close, Skye. Spread your legs, show me how wet you are."

"Thomas," I breathed.

"Skye," He groaned.

"Come for me. Come all over me. Show me how much I turn you on, how much you want me."

He let out a guttural hiss and I imagined the look on his face as he parted his lips and closed his eyes, racing to release. His whole body would tense as his cock swelled and his balls tightened. We let out a synchronised cry and he growled through the phone as he let himself go.

"Fuck," his voice was shaky as his body shuddered.

I fell into my own climax clenching around my finger as my thumb stroked my clit and I closed my legs around my hand as they spasmed.

"You've covered my hand. Both of them," I panted. "Taste my release when I slip my finger into your mouth and I'll taste yours." I sucked my finger loudly, tasting myself to show him I meant business.

"You're incredible."

"Hurry home, Baby."

"I'm leaving now."

I heard his paperwork rustling as he hung up the phone and I smiled in sated yet greedy triumph. I dressed for the party, satisfied that I had given us both an appetite for later.

When I was ready, I headed downstairs. As soon as my feet reached the ground floor, the headlights from Thomas' car shone through the frosted glass of the front door. Only the lamp by the door was on and everyone silently gathered in the foyer to wait for him. The butterflies began their dance when I heard his key in the lock and he swung the door open. I grinned when I saw he was wearing a different suit to the one he left the house in…and I would never forget the look on his face as he dropped his briefcase to the floor and looked up as we all yelled, "Surprise!"

It was a beautiful expression. In that moment, he realised he was surrounded by people who loved him. His family were there, enveloping him in the unconditional love he'd had his whole life. Everyone from the office was there; he was a good boss and he knew it, but I knew he was still shocked to see them. Joel and Chaz, his lifelong friends, were there too.

And I was there. I loved him like no one else ever would and no one would ever love me like he did.

He didn't know how to react; we had all pulled together to celebrate his birthday and I could see he was overwhelmed by the attention. When it came to business, he could command a room full of people with no qualms of self-doubt. Personally, he was like a tiger. A big, tough and almost-always horny tiger; one with a wild side and a side tamed only for me. I stepped forward, wrapped my arms around him and hugged him tightly; I had been waiting all day for his reaction and it didn't disappoint.

"Happy birthday."

He squeezed me to him and I giggled as he lifted me off my feet.

"Thank you."

I kissed him like I always did before I told him I loved him and he winked with a silent "I love you, too". I let him go and allowed his family and friends to swarm him and I spent the evening with the girls, watching the love of my life enjoy his birthday.

"Did you have fun?" I asked as we tried to tidy the house. We'd had enough to drink for the room to spin, but I couldn't go to bed until it was tidy.

"It was more than I'd ever ask for. Seriously, you did all that?"

"I did. I wanted you to have something special."

"I've got you."

"And someone else."

He shot up from kneeling on the floor and looked around.

"Who?"

"Hold on. Wait there and don't move."

I ran upstairs to the spare room to get his birthday present and my phone, and skipped down the stairs in excitement. I poked my head around the door to see him tidying up.

"Hey. I told you not to move."

"Sorry, boss," he wiggled his eyebrows, but carried on cleaning.

"Come on, this is hurting my back."

"Now who's getting old?" I gasped, but he laughed. "Just come here."

"Not until you stand up and close your eyes."

He made his way towards me and juggled the gift under one arm so I could use the other to keep him back.

"You're going to ruin it."

He stopped and sighed, but gave in and closed his eyes.

"Open," I said once I was standing in front of him.

Thomas' eyes widened in shock when they opened; it was the last thing he expected a clean freak to buy him.

"Shit."

"It will," I grinned. "And I am *not* picking it up."

"Does it have a name?"

"Buster. I adopted him from the home."

I went to the dog's home with Jenifer the week before and couldn't leave without adopting the Rottweiler puppy. He was the last of his litter and was sleeping in his basket with a little blue blanket when I saw him.

"Hey, Buster," Thomas tickled him between the ears. He took him off me and I snapped a picture as Buster licked his face. "Skye, you bought me a dog."

"I bought *us* a dog. And he's a puppy. I'll learn to deal with the mess, I just thought it would be nice to add to the family."

Thomas' eyes flew to mine. My eyes flew to his. I hadn't meant to say that. I prayed we wouldn't have to have that conversation. Thomas closed his eyes for a second and they focussed on Buster when he opened them again.

"He's the perfect addition to our family."

He didn't want to talk about it, either. I thought about it as he set the dog down and rubbed his belly. Thomas had never tried to talk about it. Hadn't most couples at least broached the subject after six years together? Maybe he didn't want children either. I didn't believe that. I'd seen him with Tommy and Jake.

Maybe he thought I'd be like my mother. That was a tough pill to swallow. Telling him about my past *had* changed things. He didn't trust me to be the mother of his children. My mind suddenly filled with visions of a little toddler with hazel brown eyes and dark hair chasing Buster around the garden.

Yeah, my system had just been well and truly shocked.

Thirty

What the hell was happening to me?
October 10th, 2010.

Buster tugged on his lead, panting wildly with excitement. We were taking a walk through the forest not far from home. Buster needed the exercise, Thomas enjoyed anything that got his heart pumping and I had to get out of the house.

Since the night of the party, I'd been suffocating in self-doubt and confusion caused by two things: the idea that, in fact, maybe I did like the idea of carrying and raising a child created by our love and the beauty and magic of science that meant we could create life…and the realisation that Thomas had written me off as a mother. Did he judge it based on how I was with Tommy and Jake? I thought I did well, considering I'd never had any interaction with small children. I loved those boys.

Maybe he judged my parenting skills based on the example set by my own parents. If that was it, I'd never change his mind. Another aspect of my life Pamela and Phillip had ruined. Thomas would forever judge me because my parents didn't stick around. I had spent the last two weeks counting down the days until my period. I even stood in the mirror a few times and imagined my belly swollen with life. I was confused. I thought I didn't want children but it was all I could think about. A pair of little shoes on the rack next to ours, a rain jacket hanging between ours, waiting for a rainy day; a Winnie the Pooh umbrella in the stand, ready to be used when we jumped in muddy puddles. Everywhere I looked, I saw proof of a life I would never have.

"You okay?"

I looked up and realised I'd stopped walking. I was standing at a pile of dry leaves, imagining running through them with a little hand held tightly in mine.

"Fine," I lied and painted on a smile. I took his hand and we walked further into the woodland.

"Shall I make us some coffee?" Thomas asked when we got in. He let Buster off his lead and he ran straight to his water bowl.

"Sure. There's some hazelnut powder in the cupboard."

"Shall we go for dinner?" He called after me as I hung my coat up and headed up the stairs.

"Sure."

Buster hopped onto the bed and watched me as I stood side on in the mirror and pushed my belly out.

"Your usual table?" The waitress asked, licking her lips like she always did when she caught sight of the man with his hand at the bottom of my back.

She led us to our candlelit table in the corner and handed us menus.

"I'll be back with your wine and water."

I watched her disappear to the back of the restaurant and wondered if her parents loved her.

"What's wrong?" Thomas held my hand across the table and I looked up at him.

"Nothing."

"Tired?"

He stroked little circles on my palm; I tried to deny the effect it had on me, but it was impossible.

"I guess."

"Shall we take a holiday?"

"We can't. We're too busy."

He sighed, "I'll drop everything and take you anywhere if it takes away that look in your eyes."

I should have known he'd read me, figure me out. It had always been that way with us.

"How about Jersey?"

"That's not the five star resort on a tropical island I was thinking of. Why Jersey?"

"We could stay with Ava and Kevin. It would be nice to relax somewhere cozy."

He frowned in suspicion.

"Are you ready to order?" The waitress returned before Thomas could question me.

"Do you really want to go to Jersey?" Thomas asked when we got home.

Dinner was nice; filled with comfortable silence and conversation. My mind had been in a constant spin for weeks and I didn't know if I was up or down, but it didn't change the way I felt about him. It only cemented the fact that I didn't deserve him. Deep down, I had always known I didn't.

"Yeah, I do. Ava and I can have some girl time, you can play golf with Kevin and we can spend some time with the boys."

Thomas pulled back the duvet as we got undressed for bed.

"I'll call Ava tomorrow and arrange a date. You're right...I think it's just what we need."

Thirty One

The best thing about being with Thomas? He knew me. He knew us. He knew just what we needed to fall in love all over again.
October 15th, 2010.

Thomas dropped our bags to the floor as we stepped into the room. I headed straight for the Juliet balcony and inhaled the salty breeze as I watched the little amber lights flicker in the distance.

"Beautiful," I turned when Thomas spoke and found him looking at me. "You're beautiful."

I smiled in gratitude. It was becoming easier to accept compliments; I believed he meant them when he gave them to me.

He tapped the sideboard next to the door and I kept my eyes on him, watching him slip off his jacket and loosen his tie as I moved across the room to sit on the cabinet. He meant what he said in the restaurant the week before; he dropped everything, left the magazine in Joel's hands and booked our ferry tickets. Nina resisted until I told her I planned to have 'the talk' with Thomas and after making me promise to appoint her godmother, she gave in. I didn't confess that I had no intention of having the talk, but it worked. I met Thomas at Waterloo Station after work and we jumped on the train to Poole.

He slid his tie out from under his collar, the silk making a harsh sound as it resisted its departure from the cotton, and he dropped it to the floor.

"You know I love you, don't you?"

He settled between my legs and placed his hands on my waist. They were the hands of a mentally and physically strong man, but also of the sweet, tender and vulnerable man only I knew.

"Yes," I answered honestly, "and I love you."

"I'm glad we've come away. It's so easy to fall into a lull at home. It's easy to lose sight of what's important."

His lips found my neck and he peppered me with kisses before he stood back and looked at me as he continued.

"You know I'd give you everything, right?"

"I do."

I reached out to unbutton his shirt, parting the cotton and pressing my hand to his heart. He wasn't talking about money or cars or holidays. He was talking about himself. I had all of him, everything he was, and it was the greatest gift I'd ever been given.

"I'd give up everything in a flash," he rested his hand over mine, "and never look back if it meant not losing you. You are all that matters. Being with you is all that matters."

I nodded. I understood, "You'll never have to do that. You're all that matters to me, too."

He dropped his gaze to where our bodies almost met and drew tiny circles on my stomach with his thumbs.

"For a long time, I thought I was disposable."

"You've never been disposable," I combed my hands through his hair until he looked at me again. "It will always be you. From the moment you pulled a rose out from behind my ear, it's been you. Maybe it always was."

"That's all I needed to know."

In a split second, all traces of vulnerability left him; he slid me off the counter, carried me across the room and placed me on the bed. I watched as he began undressing. I could have watched him forever. There was always something to marvel at; a muscle or expression that fascinated me. He cocked a brow as he slid his hands into the side of his boxers at the same time my eyes fell on the undeniable rigidity in them that made my toes curl. I sat up and quickly removed my dress. There was that look in his eyes; the one that made me want to lay beneath him and allow him to consume me, to possess me as he drank me in; every line, every curve, like he could look at me forever, too.

When I was left in nothing but the black silk ensemble he had bought me, I shimmied back on the bed, crooked my finger and beckoned Thomas to come closer.

Thirty Two

That was the day. We were always hiding from that moment on...
July 26th, 1995.

"Skye, Skye! Can I ride your new bike?"
I nodded. I wasn't really listening. I was looking around the garden for Oliver. Our friends were running around on the grass; my friends were all in pink – Oliver said pink made you look like a marshmallow.

Oliver's friends were playing football, but he wasn't there. Where was he?

I spotted him at the back of the house and wondered if he was hiding. I thought I'd sneak up on him and make him jump – I thought it would teach him for running off. We were a team. He was the one who made the team, he couldn't run off without me.

I didn't even know half of the kids at the party; Mum invited them because she wanted to make new friends. We hadn't lived in the big house long. Dad got a new job so we moved, and now we all had our own room. Beth had the attic to do her studying and have sleepovers with her friends and Oliver and I swapped rooms so I could have the one at the front with the big window and the blossom tree.

I snuck up behind him but he must have heard me. He threw his arm out to keep me back. A quick look back with his finger over his lips and I was silenced.

He was listening to something.
I listened.
I couldn't hear anything.
The kitchen sounded quiet. Maybe Oliver was playing soldiers with his friends. I could see the brownies on the counter and jumped out from behind the door to go and get one.

"Hi Mum, hi Dad."

I grabbed a brownie for me and a brownie for Oliver and left the kitchen. I shrugged when I gave it to him and left to find Rosie. She had just asked to ride my new bike. I should have said no.

Oliver ran past me and climbed the ladder for the tree house Dad had built us.

Weirdo.

Thirty Three

Shiver me timbers. Let's sail the seven seas…or the English Channel on the way to Jersey. We could have gone anywhere…nothing was removing the smile on my face.
October 16th, 2010.

"Perfect day to catch a ferry."

Thomas handed me a coffee and caged me in his arms with his hands on the railings. I turned so my back was against his front and couldn't resist the tease.

"That makes you sound old."

"I am old. Perhaps you should trade me in for a newer model."

"Not happening. You're not getting off that easy."

He kissed my neck and I rested my head on his chest.

It was a perfect day. The sky was clear and the sun was shining; it was almost too windy to hear yourself think and the water was choppy enough to turn the strongest stomachs to mush, but it was *perfect*.

Our night in the hotel was amazing. We hadn't fucked like animals and we hadn't made love. It was more than that. As his hands held mine and the rhythm of his hips sent me to paradise, we connected more than we ever had. I loved him with all my heart and if he didn't, and never would, want to start a family with me, we would always have us. It was overwhelming, the realisation that after years of rejection and loneliness, I finally believed in forever. It was because of Thomas. He made me feel alive.

"I kind of want to take you right here," he breathed in my ear, heating my blood as the cold air swept wildly around us.

Horny. He made me feel alive and horny.

"Keep it in your pants, sweetheart."

With a secret smile, I nudged my backside into him, just a little.

We said nothing as we looked out at the cloudless sky and choppy water, and stood comfortably together, like we had since Day One.

***

"AAAH!"

Ava squealed as we climbed out of the taxi and ran towards us with outstretched arms.

She hugged Thomas first as he pulled our bags from the boot and then her little arms caged me in with more strength than I expected.

"I'm so glad we're finally doing this!" She pulled me off towards the house and Thomas followed.

"Thank you for having us."

"Are you kidding?" She turned to me with infectious excitement. "When Tom called, I almost peed my pants. You'll love Jersey and the boys will be so happy to see you."

"Where are they?" I tried not to laugh, I really did, but one look back at Thomas as he shook with silent laughter and climbed the stairs with our stuff, and the laugh wanted to projectile out.

"Kev took them to play football. There's a park across the road and they go every Saturday for some boy time," she flipped the switch for the kettle. "He's been so busy at work, he hasn't seen them much lately."

"Must be tough," I tried to stop my mind wandering as Ava set about making tea and Thomas joined us in the kitchen. He gave me a kiss on the cheek and grabbed the milk from the fridge.

"Something smells good."

"I'm doing a hot buffet for lunch. It's a nice day so I thought we could sit in the garden."

"I'll make a salad."

"Oh, no you don't," she pushed him away from the sink. "No touching my kitchen."

Thomas laughed and carried on washing his hands. Ava tried to push him away. I smiled. I liked watching them together. They reminded me of Oliver and me. For the first time in a long time the pain didn't overshadow the remembrance. For the first time ever, I thought about my brother and smiled; because I missed him, because I loved him, because I knew he'd be happy for me.

"You're a guest," Ava finally managed to move him from the sink and swatted his arm when he flicked water in her face. "But you can lay the table. The boys will be back soon."

Lunch was delicious and we sat back and watched the boys on the climbing frame as we sipped Prosecco.

"Can I help you clean up?" I prepared to stand with Ava as she cleared the plates.

"No. Have another glass and relax. I'll take you into town later."

As soon as she spoke, there was a bump followed by a child's cry. We all looked up to see five-year-old Tommy running towards us with his hand on his head.

Thomas opened his arms, but the little blonde cherub stopped in front of me and tugged the sleeve of my cardigan. I panicked. What was I supposed to do?

I lifted him onto my lap and he buried his face in my neck as he cried.

"What did you do, Tommy?" I asked, aware that the adults were watching me. I didn't know why he came to me, either.

"I fell off my monkey bars," he wailed in response.

"You did? I bet you broke the floor."

He giggled through the tears, sniffed and sat up so I could sneakily check for a bump.

"Let's go see...Jake, help me see if your brother broke the floor."

Jake slid down the slide as I carried Tommy over to the climbing frame. Both boys crouched down and inspected the grass. Thank the grass lords there was a little grassless patch under the bars.

"You see?"

"Oh no!" Tommy shrieked while Jake pointed and laughed. "My head is fine now."

"I know. You're tough."

I gave his head another stroke to make sure he hadn't grown a golf ball and headed back to the table. Thomas cocked his head as he looked at me, Ava was inside and Kevin was watching the boys.

"What?" I asked when he continued to stare.

"Good job," Kevin interrupted. "He normally cries for the rest of the day."

"Sometimes distraction is the best form of comfort."

Thomas reached for my hand and I squeezed his, but I didn't need the comfort. For the first time in a long time, I wasn't hurting.

***

"Is it weird that I think of you as a sister?"

I looked up from pouring sugar in my vanilla latte to find Ava staring at me. I wondered if my warped sense of comfort and my sudden craving for a family made me imagine she had said that. I hadn't. She was looking at me like a hopeful child.

"Why would it be weird?" I smiled through the knot in my stomach and the lump in my throat.

"I always wanted a sister. Thomas was fun, but he was a goofball. We couldn't talk boys or clothes or anything else," I just nodded. I could confide in Beth *and* Oliver, about anything. "I always wanted a sister…I feel like I've found one in you."

I felt my lip tremble. I tried to control it, but I couldn't. I cried. Ava scooted her chair next to mine and wrapped her arm around me.

"I'm sorry."

I sniffed and shook my head, "It isn't bad."

I composed myself and sat up, accepting the napkin she offered me and dabbed at my eyes.

"I shouldn't have said that."

She knew, like everyone else, what I had allowed her to know. She knew I had no mother, no father, no sister; she knew I had lost Oliver. She knew I'd had him torn from me before either of us were ready to be parted from the other.

I told Thomas to tell them everything – everything *he* knew – after I met them for the first time.

"I haven't had a family for a long time. I've always wanted to feel accepted, not rejected. Thank you, Ava."

"You're part of our family now," she took my hand and squeezed. "Drink up. There's an amazing boutique I want to show you."

We walked the high street arm in arm, window shopping and talking. My phone buzzed constantly in the back pocket of my jeans, but Nina would have to get by without me. I loved the small town life Ava and Kevin had. I could imagine living there with Thomas, Buster and two or three kids.

"Ava, has Thomas ever spoken about children?"

She shrugged, "Not to me, but we don't talk about much. I know he loves the boys."

I got the feeling something wasn't right. I didn't have premonitions or the tense feeling people got before something bad happened. I didn't see my father leaving, my mother disappearing, my sister forgetting I existed, or the death of my brother coming. But I got a feeling then. I tried to quash it; I tried to push it aside – Ava hadn't said anything to trigger fear, but I was scared. Of what, I didn't know.

"Hey," she stepped in front of me and searched my face. "You okay?"

"Sure. I just wondered."

She led me off towards the afternoon market as it was closing down and the sun was beginning to set behind the old houses and shops.

"Talk to him about it," she said. "He loves you. I've never seen him so happy. If anyone can confide in him, it's you."

She rummaged in her bag for her car keys, "He's just always kind of been a closed book."

She unlocked the car and we climbed in. She pulled off towards the setting sun, in the direction of her house.

Thomas had never been a closed book with me. He told me everything. He loved me. There wasn't anything he couldn't talk to me about.

We arrived back at the house to find chicken hotpot cooked by Kevin on the table. Everyone tucked in, but all I did was watch them. Seven-year-old Jake was shovelling onions onto his brother's plate. Tommy ate them without noticing, but frowned every time he looked down and noticed his portion was the same size.

Ava was talking to Kevin about our afternoon shopping. He showed the same level of enthusiasm Thomas did when I talked shopping talk; he listened but wasn't all that interested, although I could see him mentally undressing her and wondering if she'd bought new underwear. She had. And Thomas was watching me. I couldn't let things fail. If we did one thing religiously it was communicating. We always talked, and we would…just not during our weekend in Jersey. I smiled to show him everything was fine when he gave me a questioning look. I loved it when he did that. He sucked his top lip into his mouth and frowned. He was adorable. God, I loved him.

Everything would be fine…I knew it.

Thirty Four

If pigs could fly, there'd be a sty in the sky.
October 17th, 2010.

"I don't want to go back to work," I groaned as the cab turned onto our street.

The weekend had been amazing. We'd all spent Saturday evening on the sofas in front of the gas fire while Ava and Kevin shared the boys' school stories; I had rested my head on Thomas shoulder while he held me and we listened. The weekend had been perfect, but I had felt myself slipping more than once. I zoned out, went into a trance and had no idea what I was thinking about. Kevin took Thomas to play tennis on Sunday. Thomas wasn't really a golf man and the triumphant grin and fist pump he gave me when he convinced Kevin to go to the courts instead made me smile. When they left, I sat at the garden table and watched Ava with the boys. I liked to watch. I felt like I had been on the outside looking in for a long time and, although things were different now, I liked to step back and just watch. A mother's love was a beautiful thing. I remembered when my mother loved me, like the love I saw Ava had for Tommy and Jake; I *knew* she loved me once. It was a question I would never be able to answer. Why, and how, did she just switch it off? I had convinced myself over the years that it was my fault; I must have done something wrong. I just wanted to know what I did. I would feel like a part of me was missing until I knew. I wouldn't be complete until I knew why my mother had left me, why she had become the person she became.

"You could always take some time off," Thomas said as he played with my ponytail and I closed my eyes. Why was travelling so exhausting?

"Quit my job?"

"Why not? I make enough money for the both of us."

"You weirdo. That's not the point. I'd get bored."

"Not if you kept yourself occupied," a tense silence passed between us before Thomas cleared his throat. "Imagine all the laser tag obstacles you could set up."

Yes, we liked to play laser tag in the house.

"Mmm, speaking of laser tag," I gripped his leg and ran my hands up and down his thigh. "Shall we play?"

"Laser tag?"

"I was thinking you could use a different weapon."

I licked my lips as my fingertips grazed his crotch. He tugged on my ponytail to expose my neck and dived in to sink his teeth into the flesh.

"It just so happens I'm loaded and ready to go."

I hummed in response and stroked with more pressure, feeling the arousal soak my new French knickers instantly as he grew in my hand.

"I think your holster is too small."

"It's a big weapon."

The cab pulled up outside our house. The driver looked in the rear-view mirror in shock. Brazen? Unashamed? Yes, we were.

"Go and hide."

Thomas growled as he reached into his considerably tighter pocket for his wallet and I scrambled out of the car and ran to the house. I stopped in the foyer and looked around. White blouse. Perfect.

I kicked my shoes off and left them by the door.

I shimmied out of my jeans and left them at the bottom of the stairs as I ran up.

I heard him throw our bags down as I slipped my bra out of my sleeve and hooked it over the bannister.

"Skye?"

The edge in his voice made my knees weak and I sneaked into the wet room when I heard the creak on the third stair. The water shot out of the rainfall shower and I climbed under, pulled the tie from my hair and allowed it to cascade over my shoulders with the water. The room began to fill with steam and I buzzed with anticipation.

The door opened and I looked up to find Thomas in his underwear.

"Mmm," he groaned, devouring me with those hungry eyes. "Wet shirt contest?"

"How about a white contest?"

My gaze dropped to the strain in his white boxers. His eyes fell on my shirt, my nipples visible and hard beneath the thin cotton.

He slowly stalked towards me, the steam wetting his hair so it fell over his forehead. I reached for him, pulling him under the stream and watching his glorious length appear as the underwear turned transparent.

"What now?" He cocked his brow.

A challenge.

Game on.

I dropped to my knees and pushed him back against the tiles. Hooking my fingers into his boxers, I tugged them down and caught the tip of his cock on my tongue as it sprang free. I closed my mouth just over the crown and looked up at him. I allowed a moan to vibrate down his shaft; he groaned through clenched teeth, laid his head back and slipped his hands into my hair. I sucked him into my mouth, just hard enough to make him shudder and swallowed the shot of pre-cum. Bobbing my head, I gripped the back of his thigh with one hand and held his balls in the other. I knew what he liked and I liked to drive him crazy. He eased his hips forward but I edged back, teasing him, waiting for him to lose it.

"Skye," he grunted. "Take it all."

I shook my head as I sucked up, releasing with a pop that made him quiver, and then I let the tiger loose. I took him all the way in, swallowing as he hit the back of my throat. His hips thrust forward, his hands pulled my hair and I sucked him until my eyes watered and my aching cleft throbbed with need. I felt his balls tighten and his body tense up. I sucked harder and faster, trying to not to choke, but not giving a fuck. I needed to taste him.

"Skye," he breathed, pulling my hair away from my face so he could watch his cock slide in and out of my mouth. "Skye."

He held me still as his cock jerked and he exploded. I drank every drop as it coated my tongue and slid down my throat.

"Get up."

Thomas curled his hand around my throat, pulled me to my feet and backed me up towards the opposite wall. I lost my footing so he crashed me to the tile and lifted my legs around his waist. He slammed into me and a garbled cry left my throat before his mouth attacked mine. I knew we had time; Thomas could come multiple times if he kept going and the aggression he fucked me with told me that was exactly what he intended to do. I cried out as he hooked one of my legs over his arm and pressed his hand flat to the wall. The other arm held me to him and he plunged deep into my core. I came with a scream and wrapped my arms around his neck. I came again and again, each one rippling through me like the violent waves of a deep sea storm. My legs quivered around him and my toes curled as I dug my heels into his ass.

My final orgasm hit me like a tornado and I lost my mind when he came with me, sinking his teeth into my shoulder and my body went rigid with unbearable pleasure.

The water continued to pour as I fell languidly against him and he took my weight as he set me down.

Thomas held me to him like a child as he reached for my body wash. We'd just fucked each other seven shades to Sunday, yet I'd never felt so looked after as he tenderly washed me, kissing every inch of my body until a gentle orgasm washed over me, simply from the connection and his mouth.

We were snuggled on the sofa watching the sports news. I was dressed in a t-shirt of Thomas' and the pair of boy shorts he'd picked out, and he was in his boxers and glasses, entranced by the news so he knew what was going on in the sports world before work the next day.

"The boxing heavyweight title is on the line next Saturday as Bloodhound Brett goes up against The Cyclone to try and knock him off the podium..." the newsman continued reeling off the news, but I was lost as they cut to highlights of the last match between the two fighters. I sat up on the edge of the sofa.

Curtis was on TV, in a suit, standing by the ring with a stoic, emotionless expression on his beautiful face.

"Thomas-" I pointed to the screen, but there was a knock at the door before I could speak.

"Who's that?" He prepared to stand, but I beat him to it.

"I'll go. It's probably Jen bringing Buster back."

I needed air. Maybe opening the door would give me the smack in the face I needed to get my heart going again.

I opened the door and froze.

"Hi, Skye."

"Beth."

Thirty Five

Holy. Mother. Fuck.
October 17th, 2010.

I didn't know what to say. I couldn't say anything. I just stared at my big sister as she stared at me. She was smiling like we hadn't been strangers for the last ten years. She was gorgeous; I was able to register that much. She looked like our father; pale skin, dark hair, golden eyes that weren't quite green or brown. She looked like me. I looked like my father. It was too much to take in.

"Are you going to invite me in?" She smiled. We even had the same teeth. It was like looking in a mirror and seeing myself in five years, except she was thinner than me. I carried a little extra weight; probably payback for the popcorn and Nutella I'd eaten while my world fell apart around me.

I felt like that again as I continued to stare. The walls I'd build between the past and present came tumbling down. The collision of times was never supposed to happen.

I could smell the smoke. I could hear the shouting. I felt the reminder of loneliness; it fell on me like a ton of bricks.

"Skye?" She was still there.

"What are you doing here?"

"I lost you," she whispered. "Two years ago. My phone was stolen and I lost you."

"It's been seven years, Beth."

"I know," she took a step forward, but I took one back. "Please, just let me in."

"Skye?" Thomas appeared at the door. "Oh."

He knew. It was impossible not to. Even the blind could have seen we were related.

"Hello," She was waiting for an introduction. She wasn't going to get one.

"I think you should leave."

"Skye," both Beth and Thomas said.

I was contemplating changing my name.

"It's fine," I pushed Thomas back and closed the door around me before turning to Beth. "I needed you. I needed you then, when I had nothing else."

"I'm sorry."

"We had no one, Beth. *I* had no one. We were supposed to face it together, but you ran away like everyone else."

"Skye-"

"No," I shook my head. "I can't. You need to leave."

I closed the door and my heart fell. As I turned around and leaned against the door for some much needed support, I saw Thomas sitting on the bottom step waiting for me.

I knew the pain I saw in his eyes mirrored mine. So I did it for him. I turned around and opened the door.

"Beth?"

She stopped still at the edge of the driveway and bowed her head. Was she waiting for an onslaught of abuse and expletives? I didn't know. I only knew one thing – the words that would come next.

"Come in."

Thomas disappeared into his office as I led Beth into the house and through to the lounge. I stood by the door as she walked around the room, looking over the various photos of our holidays.

"What's his name?" She asked, picking up a photo of us in Egypt.

"Thomas."

"You're married?"

"No. We have everything. We don't need a couple of rings and a party."

"But you're wearing a ring."

She looked at the diamond and ruby ring on my finger and I covered it with my other hand.

"Thomas gave it to me. It's a promise ring," I couldn't help the bitterness in my voice. "He promised he'd never leave me."

He bought it for me on our first anniversary. My birthday. We weren't just celebrating a year together. He was helping me to heal and be able to celebrate my birthday again. I would never forget that night for as long as I lived. It was the first time he told me he loved me. It was the first night I let him in. It was the night he promised he'd always be there for me, and love me like no other. Every day since then, he seemed to love me more.

"I'm glad you have him."

"He's all I've got."

Beth moved to the mantelpiece. I wanted to scream like a feral beast when she picked up Oliver's photo, but I calmed when she caressed the silver frame and traced her fingers over the letters of his name. The tears built and my heart thawed just a little as she stroked her thumb over his face and held the photo to her chest.

She missed him.

"I think about you every day. Both of you."

"What happened?"

"I think I was ashamed. I was away when Dad left but I thought things would work out. Then – then Oliver died and I wasn't there. I should have been there. When Mum disappeared, it all just fell apart."

She sat down and buried her face in her hands before continuing.

"You were the strong one and you were just a baby. You lost, but you battled to survive and look where you are now," she looked up as the tears fell. "I ran and I pretended it wasn't happening. I didn't even grieve. I just told myself Oliver had moved away."

I fell to the sofa opposite and just looked at her; it was all I could do. I couldn't say anything. What was there to say that would ease the pain that had quickly consumed us both?

"I'm getting married," she kept her eyes on her lap where her fingers were now knotted together. "You know, with a couple of rings and a party."

She tried to laugh, but I stayed quiet. I was suspicious.

"I can't start a family knowing I deserted mine because I was a coward."

"So this is about easing a guilty conscience?"

"No," she shot to her feet. "It's about trying to fix everything. I just want my family back."

"We're not a family anymore."

"But we can be."

I scraped my hands through my hair, and remembered my state of undress.

"Look," I sighed. "It's late. I can't do this now. Stay here tonight and we'll talk tomorrow."

Thomas swooped into the room like the saint he was.

"Beth, I've set up the spare room for you."

"Thank you."

"It's down here. Third door on the right. You've got your own bathroom and you can take anything you need from the kitchen and utility room."

"Thank you, Thomas. I'm sorry we're meeting like this."

"Maybe there will be more smiles over breakfast," he offered her a weak smile and turned to me. "I'll meet you in bed."

"Don't steal from me," I said to Beth when he'd gone. "And don't run. If you run, we're done for good."

I left her standing in the middle of the lounge. She could stew. She could wonder if things were going to be okay. I'd been doing it for years.

I climbed the stairs heavily. My heart hurt. I had no idea what to do. It was like one of those dreams you'd been waiting for, only to find it was a nightmare.

I smelled the lavender and closed my eyes as the calming scent filled my nostrils.

I entered the bedroom and found tea lights flickering on the chest of drawers and bedside cabinets. I sighed as I looked at Thomas, standing by the bed waiting for me.

"What did I do to deserve you?"

I could feel the emotion bubbling not far under the surface. Thomas saw it.

He strode towards me and placed his hands on my shoulders, "You breathed."

He crushed me to him and I cried into his chest, great loud sobs of regret and fear of the future.

"Hey," he held me back and wiped the tears away with his thumbs. "I'm here. I'll never let anyone hurt you." I nodded. "Come."

He led me to my side of the bed and tapped my arms for me to raise them. Removing his t-shirt from my body, he kissed each shoulder and pulled back the duvet as he discarded the cotton on the floor.

"On your stomach."

I got on the bed with a sigh and relaxed a little more. The mattress dipped as he straddled me and the smell of lavender grew stronger.

"You're still clothed," I said, turning my head to look at him.

"It's not about sex," he squirted oil onto his hands. "Just relax and let me take care of you."

His hands found my shoulders and began to ease the tension that had knotted at the bottom of my neck the second the news came on, and as he slowly caressed my body, encouraging the tightness and aching to fuck off, I closed my eyes.

As I drifted into a Thomas and lavender induced sleep, my mind travelled back, and back some more.

Thirty Six

I was lucky to have a brother like Oliver.
June, 1997.

"Skye!"
I turned around to see Oliver chasing after me. The girls I was with fluttered their eyelashes and – far too indiscreetly – pushed out their chests. They always did that when Oliver was around. They were all crushing on my brother and, as much as I told them how awkward that was for me, they didn't stop. Oliver was tall, taller than me at least, with dark hair that flopped across his forehead and bumfluff on his face that he wouldn't shave no matter how many times I'd laughed at it. What the other girls saw, I had no idea. He was my brother; I had to listen to him burp and watch him scratch his butt on the way to the bathroom in the mornings. He was kind of brooding, I guessed; he was always on guard, watching, like he was waiting for something.

"Yes?" I huffed when he caught up to us.
"Can we go to the library?"
If anyone else on the face of the earth had said that, the girls would have turned their noses up and walked away, but when Oliver said it, they swayed on their feet like they were leaves on a tree blowing in the breeze.

"Really?" I whined. "Why?"
"I have some stuff to do and I can't do it at home. I'll help you with your homework if you need it."
"Maybe we could all go. I'm sure you're a great teacher," Clara suggested, her voice sounding nothing like the one she swore at me, frequently, with.

"It's okay," Oliver grabbed the strap of my bag and pulled me from the group. "You're probably getting better grades than me, anyway. See you later, girls."

They all sighed like the teens in those Fifties movies as we headed back into school and to the library.

"What's the deal?" I asked, pulling out of Oliver's hold. "You never want to study with me."

"Sure I do," he looked at me with a cheesy grin. "You're my little sister."

"You never let me forget it."

I returned his grin and opened the library door.

I did have work to do. Mr White, the headmaster, was my science teacher but he had to step out of the day's class because one of the older boys had been in a fight.

I pulled my text books out of my bag and got to work. I could finish the lesson's exercise while Oliver did his work and we would be home in time for dinner.

I looked up from my workbook when I was finished. Oliver was leaning back in his chair with his headphones on and eyes closed. The journal he carried everywhere with him was resting on his chest. I kicked him under the table to get his attention.

"Are you done?" He asked, slipping the headphones around his neck.

"Yep. I thought you had work to do?"

He looked down and began packing his Walkman away.

"You know we're a team, don't you? You and me?"

"Of course, crazy. Why?"

"I just want to make sure you know it."

I nodded and we stood up and left the library. We waved to the caretaker as he walked the hallways swinging his keys around his finger. We must have been in the library for ages.

Oliver took my bag off me and swung his arm over my shoulder. I swatted him away when he started messing up my ponytail.

"You know I'll protect you, don't you? Whatever it is, whoever it is, I'll protect you. Don't ever think you can't talk to me...about anything. *Just promise me you know that.*"

"I know," *I jumped up to throw my arm around his shoulder and walked on tiptoes.* "You're my big brother."

I messed up Oliver's hair and laughed when he playfully shoved me away.

Thirty Seven

I didn't trust Beth as far as I could throw her. And the return of my estranged big sister wasn't the only thing on my mind.
October 18th, 2010.

I slept like I was in a coma but woke up an hour early and felt awful. Thomas wasn't in bed; I could smell his body wash from the shower and he'd left his wardrobe doors open like he always did.

I heaved myself out of bed, into the bathroom and skulked downstairs. I heard Beth and Thomas talking. I'd almost forgotten about her. Almost. Thomas was leaning against the counter with his protein shake and a granola bar. It was gym day. Beth was sitting at the breakfast bar with a cup of coffee.

"Good morning," Thomas handed me my cup as I stepped into his arms. "I called Nina."

"Thomas, I'm going to work."

"I told you she was tameable," he grinned. "You've got the week off."

I rolled my eyes, "Great."

He tipped the remains of his shake in the sink, washed it down and grabbed my hand as he pulled his jacket off the back of the stool.

"Bye, Beth," she waved as he led me out of the room. "Get out of the house with her today. Let her talk and just listen."

"When did you become an agony aunt?" I gripped his jacket when he'd put it on and straightened it. I didn't want him to leave.

"I like to think I know what you need," he kissed my forehead and pried my hands away. "It'll be okay. I'll call you at lunch. I love you."

"I love you too."

Thomas opened the door and Jen was standing on the other side with a wriggly Buster in her arms. Thomas kissed her cheek as he stepped past and waved to me before he got in his car.

"Hi, Jen," I took Buster off her. "Thanks for having him."

"He likes socks," she sighed and held up a pair of chewed up old football socks. "I'm guessing you don't want a lift to work?"

She nodded at my t-shirt and tried not to laugh. Yes, I lived in my boyfriend's clothes.

"Family stuff. I'll call you later."

She nodded, sensing the unease. I did finally tell the girls about everything – almost everything – pre-2003; I couldn't keep avoiding answering the questions about what I was doing for Mother's Day or where I was spending Christmas. I told them I was a twin – used to be a twin. I told them Oliver had died in an accident; I didn't tell anyone how. I couldn't relive the past and see the images in my mind when I told people what happened. I hadn't even been able to tell Thomas. I told them I had no parents, using the pity that I detested to my advantage. People weren't insensitive enough to probe, so I got away with telling them the bare minimum – enough to stop the questions.

"Sure thing," she scratched Buster's head and gave me half a hug. "If you need anything, call me, okay?"

"Thank you. Enjoy covering for me."

She clapped her hands in excitement and skipped to her car. She wanted my job. She'd been at Poise as long as I had and was the office manager. She couldn't go any higher until one of the bosses needed a PA, and she wanted to work alongside Nina. Everyone did. I put in a good word with the fiery divorcee and Jen covered for me whenever I was off. I closed the door as she honked her horn – at 7.30am – and pulled away.

Beth. I sighed. How was I supposed to deal with her?

I dropped Buster to the floor and he sniffed her out as I headed back into the kitchen. She was still sitting at the breakfast bar, picking at her nail polish.

"Can you make sure the specks go in the bin please?"

"Sure."

She picked her nails when she was nervous; always had done. I hated it. So did Oliver.

"What do you want to do today?" I asked as I opened the fridge and stared in. I didn't know what to do with myself.

"Can we talk?"

"Yes," I pulled out some orange juice. "But not here. This house is our sanctuary and I can't face the past here."

"I don't want to be your past, Skye."

"Go and shower and get ready. I need an hour to do some work and we'll go out."

I took my juice to the lounge and switched on the news. The presenter reeled of the football league tables while I emailed Nina to apologise and asked for some work to do at home. I didn't want to be alone in the house for a week. I'd kept myself busy, non-stop, for years.

The fight. It was on TV again; the same clips as last night replaying. Curtis.

I slid off the sofa and crawled towards the TV, sitting as close as I could. He didn't look how I remembered. He used to be so full of charisma, but all I saw in his eyes then was sadness. He hadn't found the happiness he deserved. After all those years, I still hurt for him. I didn't know about his past, not like he knew about mine, but I saw the burden. I *felt* it. And I knew he was alone – like I had been before I found Thomas. Alone and afraid, but putting on a brave face. His charcoal suit hid his tattoos and his hair was considerably longer than it used to be. He looked older; the same stress lines on his face I saw on Geoff's the night I met him. I hated that I could see him and he had no idea. I hated that he saw me and ran. I hated that it *was* him on New Year's Eve and I let him go. I knew how it felt to need a friend when it was impossible to let someone in. I hated that he was still alone. He deserved to be happy, to move on from the past that had tormented us both.

"Skye?"

Beth caught me with my face inches from the TV screen and the news had moved on to golf.

"Yeah," I cleared my throat as I got to my feet. "I like golf."

I hated golf.

***

"Come on Buster."

I opened the back door of the car and he jumped out and sat by my feet. Thomas was a genius. In just three weeks, he'd trained our little Rottweiler puppy; he might have liked to chew on socks, but he waited for my permission to move. Ducks quacked, trees rustled in the breeze and the water sloshed nearby, but Buster stayed right by me.

I'd brought us to the lakes. It was an open space that would, hopefully, allow me to breathe during what was bound to be a tough conversation.

"Go on."

Buster walked slightly ahead as we walked to a bench near the water and I threw him a toy as we sat down. He ran off to the shallows shaking the rabbit toy from side to side.

"So you're getting married."

"I am."

"And he knows you're here?"

"I've told Jack everything. I haven't sugar-coated or made excuses," she picked at her nail polish again. "He proposed a few months ago. I told him I can't marry him until I've fixed all of my mistakes."

"We all make mistakes. We can't fix them all."

"We can fix the ones that matter."

"I don't understand why it matters now," Buster brought his toy over and I threw it back out for him. "We've had years to fix this."

"Life is too short. We lost our brother with no choice. We have the chance to get each other back."

"It's not that easy. Too much has happened. I mean, what do you expect to happen now?"

"I don't know. Phone calls, lunches, family dates. I just want my sister back."

"I've never not wanted my sister."

"Just give me time, Skye," she caught Buster's toy and threw it back before he arrived at the bench and covered us in mud. "If there's one thing we don't know, it's how much time we've got left."

"I know."

I thought about that every day. Would I find out if Dad died? Would someone tell me if Mum died? If I died tomorrow, had I said and done everything that deserved to be said and done?

"What about Mum and Dad?" I asked.

"Nothing. I saw Dad when I went home looking for you. He said he'd call, but he hasn't."

"And Mum?"

"Nothing."

"That sucks."

Deep down, I hoped they would have tried to find us. They were the only ones who had wrongs to right.

"I'm sorry."

"Me too," I nodded. "Will you stay for a while?"

"I'm not going anywhere. Never again."

"I just don't get it. We had everything. There was nothing we couldn't talk about."

She bowed her head but I couldn't stop.

"For years, *years,* I thought it was me. I thought I'd done something to make everyone leave. You and Oliver and I were best friends, the three musketeers, and you left us. Both of us."

The cold began to chill my bones and I shivered, but the anger didn't stop. I was supposed to be listening, not talking, but the pent up anger, and hurt and fear flowed from my lips venomously. I shoved my hands in my pockets and paced back and forth in front of the bench. Beth just watched.

"Do you have any idea how it felt?" I didn't look for her reaction, keeping my eyes on the ground and kicking up the dirt. "Do you know how much I had to fight, just to kill the urge to give up?" I looked at her then, as her sorrowful eyes met mine. "I'm not trying to make you feel bad. Just don't think you can turn up here, call yourself a coward and everything will snap back into place."

"I'm just asking for a second chance."

"I can give you that. But I'm no longer the poor hungry teenager you left behind."

***

Beth was a self-employed estate agent. She owned her own company and had invested enough money into shares programs so that, at thirty one, she could retire and never have to worry. And she could cook. Nina sent over some stuff for me to archive on my week off, so while I locked myself in Thomas' office to pull apart PDFs, Beth cooked an amazing beef stroganoff.

Thomas came home to dinner on the table. I loved gym days; he did enough cardio to burn off the midnight snacks he tried keep secret, and lifted enough weights to stay…buff. I loved to try and get both hands around his biceps when he came in, but I substituted it for a subtle squeeze with Beth being present.

"Ever thought about being a chef?" Thomas asked as he tucked in.

"Jack eats a lot. I had to learn to cook to snag him," she twisted her ring around her finger. "How did you two meet?"

"Margarita Monday." We said with a shared look of gratitude.

"What?"

"He pulled a rose from behind my ear in Jose's alleyway and I've been his ever since."

"Skye can't turn down a magic trick," she chuckled and leaned on her elbows. "You know, when we were kids, Skye was obsessed with magic. She begged Mum and Dad to take her to see a show and was ready to kick the illusionist's butt when he pulled out the saw and attempted to cut his assistant in half."

"I know," Thomas shrugged and squeezed my knee under the table. I'd told him that story before; it was a fond childhood memory, but as his hand moved higher, neither of us were thinking about *that* magic trick.

"You're cute together."

We turned and smiled at each other, like we did every time someone said that. We just fit. It was one of the most beautiful things about our relationship. He was hot – I know, I was biased. And I was…curvy. But we fit like a jigsaw. We rarely got looks from strangers that wondered why one of us was with the other. Not that it mattered; he was my caveman no matter what anyone else thought.

We finished dinner and Thomas and I washed the dishes before we all retired to the lounge to finish our second bottle of wine.

"Why don't you ask Jack over for dinner Friday night, Beth?" Thomas suggested as he stroked the back of my neck.

Good idea.

"It would be nice to meet him."

"It isn't too soon?" She asked and we immediately shook our heads.

"Jump in at the deep end."

"Thank you."

I wasn't sure if I trusted her. It was something that would be built with time. And that's what we had. It took me a while to let people in, but I had to forgive her and I had to try and forget, for Oliver, if not for myself. He loved us both and we owed it to him to try and repair what had been broken.

Thirty Eight

It was kind of how I imagined I'd act if I ever went bungee jumping....Just close your eyes, take a deep breath and jump. October 21st, 2010.

Thomas and I had wrapped up warm and taken Buster for a late night walk, heading straight to bed when we got back. We climbed under the duvet and I laid on my back as Thomas laid on his side, propped his head up with his elbow and ran his fingertips up and down my stomach with his other hand.

"Thank you."

"What for?"

"For being you," I brushed his hair back from his forehead. "I never thank you for everything you do for me."

"I do it because I want to. I want the best for you...I want you to be happy."

"I know," I stopped and thought for a minute. "I can talk to you about anything right? And know that it won't change the way you feel about me?"

"Always."

Not one witty thought entered my mind as I tried to plan what to say. I was terrified. Remember the crossroads? I was there again, only this time I had no choice; one way was blocked. If I chose that path, our relationship was over. I had to choose the open path – the one with no road signs; the one that gave no hint of where it led. I jumped with a silent scream because I didn't know if Thomas would catch me or let me fall.

"I-" I stopped and choked on the nerves as the tears filled my eyes. I was close, so close, to regressing and pushing him away.

He parted his lips as his panic matched mine.

"What's going on?"

"I want...I think I want a baby."

He let out a gush of air and collapsed back on the bed. He closed his eyes and took a few deep breaths. That was it. It had to be over.

"That's what you've wanted to talk about for weeks?"

"Weeks?"

"You've been sitting on this for a while."

I slid away from him as his eyes opened. They were glassed over; he was emotional. It was about to happen…the "I can't have a baby with you" confession. What had I done?

"It isn't an impulsive thing," I answered defensively and cleared my throat. My voice was failing with my gumption. "I'm sorry."

"Baby," I flinched as he reached for me and pulled me into him. "I thought you didn't want children."

"I don't…I want children with you."

He turned his head so his face was so close, his warm breath tickled my lips, travelled over my cheeks and swept down my neck.

I shivered, "It's okay that you don't want them with me. But we need to talk. Our honesty is the most important thing to me."

"I love you so much," he smiled and shook his head. "Having kids isn't a bad thing."

"It's not?"

He sat up against the headboard and I rested my head on his lap, shifting so I could look up at him.

"No."

"But my parents. They – well, they…" I trailed off. I couldn't say it.

"You think I don't want a family with you because of your parents?" I nodded. "You crazy, crazy woman. I haven't even thought about that."

"You haven't?"

My nerves were slowly easing. I thought he'd written me off like all the others had. I could tell by that tender, cautious look in his eye that he hadn't.

"No. I've never been a parent either. I don't know how it works. We'll learn together."

"Okay," My brain switched into rewind. "Wait, what?"

"Let's start a family."

My mouth fell open. I didn't try to disguise my shock. My heart raced. My hands squeezed into fists as Thomas resumed his pattern on my stomach and then pressed his hand over my bellybutton.

"Okay…Let's start a family."

Every aspect, every area of my life had been a constant battle. I was expecting a fight; to have to give up every ounce of dignity I had to try and convince Thomas that I wouldn't make an awful mother. I didn't know what kind of mother I would make, but I knew I would fight for our family and love it with all my heart.

Thomas, a father. Me, a mother. A little baby that needed patience and milk at ungodly hours. A toddler that would require more patience while it threw tantrums worse than any PMSing she-beast, but would give the best cuddles in the world.

I didn't know what kind of team we'd be, but we'd be one full of love, fight and goofball Kodak moments.

***

Beth was nervous. She'd painted her nails just so she could pick it off and I was damn near growing a hernia trying to contain the urge to pry her hands apart.

Why was she nervous? How much of a villain had she made herself out to be? Or did she actually play the victim? I guessed she was both; we both were. I could have tracked her down. I could have made more of an effort. I shut my friends out; maybe I did the same to Beth and made her feel like the bad guy. But it wouldn't do either of us good dwelling on it – we were different people than we were back then. The past, no matter how much it still hurt, had to be archived and locked in that little box labelled 'history'.

To hell with it; we were going to enjoy her night.

"Pick a band, any band," I called from the lounge. Beth was in the kitchen preparing dinner and I was standing in front of Thomas' dock. The day after his party, we'd taken forever transferring his horde of music CDs to his iPod.

"Bon Jovi."

Good choice, sister. I hit shuffle on Bon Jovi and good ol' Jon blasted through the speakers as I danced my way back to the kitchen. Thomas and I danced all the time. Like idiots, I might add. That much was clear when I saw the shock and shame on Beth's face. Yes, I had about as much rhythm as a one-legged. Still, I danced; banging my head, playing my air guitar and singing, "It's my life, it's now or never!"

Beth shook her head, but I saw her tapping her foot and chopping carrots to the beat as I jumped around the breakfast bar. My hair was a tangled mess as it swung from side to side.

"Come on, Beth!"

She looked over her shoulder as she began wiggling her hips and then she spun around and belted the chorus with me, throwing her tea towel in the air and jumping on the spot like she was on a pogo stick. The song finished and we threw our arms around each other. Music made everything better. Music or dancing. Dancing like an idiot. That might have been it…but the tension had gone and the nervousness had crawled back into the hole it had escaped from. And Beth still shook her butt as she went back to preparing vegetables.

I turned around to find Thomas standing in the doorway with his arms, those arms, folded.

"How long have you been there?"

He pulled out his air guitar and bent backwards, throwing his head back as he played.

"That long, huh?" I stepped into his arms and we danced together.

"Long enough to record it," he wiggled his eyebrows, those eyebrows, and pulled out his phone to record us.

I kissed him on the cheek and we sang a few lines together.

Thomas continued recording as I threw my hands in the air and danced next to Beth.

"Put that thing away and go and shower."

He shoved his phone in his pocket, but instead of leaving the room he chased me around the island, caught me and threw me over his shoulder.

"Shower time," he shrugged as Beth laughed, then smacked my ass and carried me up the stairs.

Dinner was ready when we got back downstairs and I gave Beth an apologetic look. We were used to not having to think about anyone else. She waved her hand in dismissal and handed us a glass of wine.

"Thanks," Thomas walked around the kitchen with his nose in the air. Exactly like Buster was doing at the same time. "What's cooking?"

"Roast pork," Beth swatted him away. "And no, you can't taste it until it's on your plate in front of you."

"She's figured me out," he threw his arm over her shoulders and sniffed some more.

Was it possible that everything was going to be okay? Thomas and Beth got on like they'd known each other for longer than three days. If I didn't have him, I wouldn't even have let her in. She may never have found me; I'm sure whatever came up on Google that included my name had something to do with Thomas. It was kind of funny, that I believed in fate. Being with him showed me, without a doubt, that it existed. I'd found it. Fate personified in Thomas Radley.

The doorbell rang and Buster barked and scurried to the door, ready to protect. Thomas and Beth stopped nodding their heads to the music and Beth looked at me.

"It's for you."

I turned the music down in the kitchen as we waited for her.

"Tell me it's going to be okay."

I suddenly needed reassurance. It was really happening. We were about to introduce one world to another and if it ended badly, it would be painful. I'd already jumped on the pain train willingly once and got thrown off. I couldn't do it again.

"It'll be okay," he pulled me into him and my heart set racing for an entirely different reason. "You want to know why?"

"Why?"

"Because we've got us."

He was right; of course he was. We could face anything if we faced it together.

Beth stepped into the kitchen as we made our way out, and Jack was just behind her. He was exactly what I expected; light hair – Beth always liked guys with light hair. He was taller than Thomas with a chiselled jaw and light green eyes and as he smiled and held out his hand to Thomas and me, I knew he was The One for Beth.

"Hi Jack," I took his hand. "Nice to meet you."

Thirty Nine

It had taken years, but finally, things were looking brighter. Every cloud, right?
Christmas Day, 2010.

Thomas wrapped his arms around me, set his hands on my stomach and rested his head on my shoulder. Moving us both to the music, he inhaled the scent of the cooking soup and hummed in appreciation.

"What do you need me to do?"

"Bread," I pointed to the cupboard by the stairs. "The bread is proofing."

He blew a raspberry on my neck and I shrieked and flicked soup everywhere. He got me every time. His laugh gave me butterflies as I turned and watched him walk away.

We were hosting Christmas. I never thought I'd see the day, and strangely, I wasn't as tempted to run away as I thought I would be. I wasn't praying for time machines or teleportation. I was ready for Christmas. I had everything organised and a man not afraid to use his hands in the kitchen. The past couple of weeks had been tough. Christmas was always a bittersweet time. I didn't think there would ever be a Christmas where there wasn't some degree of melancholy, but I tried to embrace it and stay calm. The mess made me antsy, and I'd started my period that morning. I had stopped taking the pill in October, but I guessed it took a while. I was trying to stay relaxed over that, too.

Beth and Jack arrived first, with Christmas pudding and black forest gateaux; Fran and Martin arrived just ahead of Ava and Kevin and brought the stuffing – it was Fran's mother's recipe so she insisted on making it – and Ava and Kevin brought a bunch of flowers and a bottle of brandy.

Tommy and Jake flew to Thomas like they always did and I was left with the dinner when he took the boys, and the men, upstairs to the games room. He had added a pinball machine and giant scalextric just for Christmas. I wasn't alone for long; the women joined me in the kitchen and looked for things to do. Beth was the first one to pick up a broom and I sagged with relief.

We decided to have dinner before opening gifts so we all sat at the table in the dining room and Thomas and I served up my carrot and coriander soup and his bread rolls.
"Before we start," Thomas stood and shushed the boys. "I just want to say thank you for coming. A lot has changed over the past few months and as a result, we have a family. Skye and Beth finally have the family they deserve, and we have been blessed with them." He squeezed my shoulder and I held my breath to stop the emotion escaping. He raised his glass. "To family."
"To family."
He sat back down and the table erupted into laughter as the boys jumped into their soup and it afforded Thomas and I a while to let it sink in. Things really were looking better than they ever had.
Merry Christmas, Oliver.

Forty

I guess I should have seen it. I should have read the signs...But I thought we were a happy family.
Christmas Day, 2001.

Beth and I helped Mum in the kitchen. She kind of just barked orders and sipped on Advocaat while we did as we were told. Oliver was watching TV, but that didn't last long; Mum quickly pulled him into the kitchen to help.

"I know you're a man," she snorted. "But don't think you don't have to pull your own weight around here."

"Where's Dad?" He rolled his eyes and looked around the kitchen for something to do.

Dad had disappeared not long after we opened our presents. He slipped away while Oliver and I were talking about the track lists on the back of our CDs and Beth was swooning over her Westlife calendar.

"Do you see him here?" She popped another cube of ice in her drink and peered over my shoulder.

"No."

"Then it doesn't matter."

Dad came home just as we sat down to eat. It was usually his job to carve the turkey but Oliver had already done it.

"Good job, son," he ruffled his hair and sat at the other end of the table. "Looks good."

"We all chipped in," Beth said, proud of our hard work. We worked well as a team.

Oliver glared at Mum, then at Dad. I don't know why it bothered him as much as it did. Dad always had to work. It had been that way for as long as I could remember.

"Who made the gravy?"

"Me."

"It's good, Sunshine."

I smiled back when Dad smiled at me. He always called me Sunshine. He said when I was born, three minutes after Oliver, the sun peered out from behind the clouds and shone into the delivery room. He said that's why they named me Skye.

"I made it how you showed me."

He nodded slowly as he pursed his lips; a sign that he was impressed, and we all bowed our heads for him to say grace.

Mum didn't say much over dinner. She didn't say anything, actually; she just ate her dinner and sipped her drink, only speaking to ask for more vegetables while we talked with Dad, discussing taking a holiday when Beth came home from university in the spring.

Dad didn't pour brandy over the Christmas pudding when it was time for dessert. I think he had noticed, like we had, that Mum had had too much. He cut the pudding and slid the custard across the table with our bowls. He dug his spoon into his pudding and paused before pulling his phone out of his pocket, looking at the screen and frowning, perplexed.

"Work," *he shrugged, shoving his chair back and standing from the table.* *"I'll be back."*

He kissed us all on the top of the head and as the door opened and closed, silence fell over the table. Mum poured another drink and stared at Dad's empty seat.

Forty One

Tick-tock, tick-tock, tick-tock, tick-tock.
January, 2011.

Thomas insisted we leave the house for the day. We took Buster for a relaxing walk round the lake and dropped him off home before we went for lunch at our usual Sunday spot; a beautiful riverside restaurant not far from home.
"How are you feeling?" He asked, filling our glasses with iced water.
"Good. I feel good."
"No change?"
He held his hand out palm-up and I placed my hand on top.
"I don't think so. We can check in a couple of weeks."
"I'm excited."
I smiled. I could see it in his eyes; he wanted it as much as I did and I wanted a baby more than anything. What had I been worried about? We had a long road ahead of us but, for once, the unknown was not scary, but exciting.
"So am I," I confessed with confidence. "But if it doesn't happen, it doesn't change anything."
"Of course it doesn't," he kissed the inside of my wrist and leaned over to kiss my lips. "Why would you think that?"
"I don't. I just don't want us to be disappointed if it takes a while."
"Baby, we've got a lot of life left. I'd wait forever for this."
"Me, too."
My phone rang as the waiter arrived. I excused myself from the table and left Thomas to order for me as I stepped out onto the terrace.
"Hi, Nina," I sighed. "What's wrong now?"

She had already called three times since we'd been out. Thomas didn't like it; he made that clear. I didn't like it either. It was Sunday. Sunday was our day.

"I don't like the cover. It hasn't been edited properly."

"They're being printed tomorrow Nina. We've run out of time."

"There's always enough time."

I knew there wasn't and she knew there wasn't, but as usual she wanted her own way.

"I like the cover. So did you when you finalised it," I reassured her. "It's bold, it's eye-catching and the model is beautiful. You're worrying about nothing."

"Are you sure?" She let out a loud breath.

"I'm sure. Don't worry."

"Thank you."

"It's okay. I have to go, Thomas is waiting. The magazine is going to sell, maybe even better than usual."

"You're right," she sighed and I felt the energy change as she composed herself. "Now, go and give that handsome man of yours a kiss from me."

I laughed. "Goodbye, Nina."

I hung up the phone and headed back inside. I watched Thomas from the door as he played with the flower petals of the centrepiece. He was my man. Self-assured, confident and hot-as-hell; funny, adorable and an animal. I finally believed I deserved everything he gave me. I strode over to him, my heels clicking on the floor. That drew his eyes to find me just as I stopped at the table and bent to kiss him. It caught him by surprise; it surprised me how much I needed to kiss him in that moment, not caring who saw us. I slipped my hand into the back of his hair, my other hand rested on the table and I kissed Thomas like it was the first time.

"What was that for?" He asked with a champion smile when I freed him and sat back in my chair.

"Nina sent a kiss. I thought I better make it a good one."

"Oh, you did," he winked. "Nina can call more often if she sends kisses like that."

"Cheeky." I grinned.

"You know it," he said with a slight head shake.

I shook my head and we sat in silence, the hustle and bustle of Sunday lunch disappearing.

***

"Babe, I don't think we need that many vegetables."

Thomas had decided to join me for the weekly grocery shop. He usually stayed at home and worked while I wandered around the supermarket with my earphones in, but he drove us there and was throwing enough vegetables in the trolley to feed an army of rabbits.

"We need to be eating healthily."

God, I loved him. I would never get bored of telling myself, and him, that. I loved that he took care of me. He had stopped drinking with me; wine with dinner had been replaced with homemade strawberry and basil water from Fran, or lemonade Thomas had made when we got home from work. Fatty foods and dinners at our favourite Italian restaurant had been replaced with grilled meat and vegetables. Our lifestyle had changed while we prepared for our baby and I had never felt healthier. I had never been happier.

"We are," I stopped him, wrapped my arms around his waist and tipped my head back for a kiss. He obliged and I smiled as I let him go and began going through what he'd put in the shopping trolley. "If we need more, we'll come and get it but if we buy all this now, we'll have to throw most of it away."

"I didn't think of that."

"It's okay," I bumped my hip into his. "You're a man."

"You're playing the gender card?"

"I sure am. Women are better shoppers. It's in our genes."

He threw his head back and laughed, drawing attention from other shoppers, "I'll remember that next time I walk past Victoria's Secret."

"Ouch. You wound me, Thomas. I'll be too big to wear it when we've conceived anyway."

"Never," he slipped his hand into the back pocket of my jeans and squeezed. "I can't wait to have more of you to hold onto."

"Then you should probably stop feeding me rabbit food."

He covered his heart with his hand, "Now who's doing the wounding?"

"All in good fun, sweetheart."

I threw some bananas in the trolley and added a little swish to my hips knowing he was watching.

"Can we buy one?" Thomas grabbed the waistband of my jeans and pulled me to a stop.

We were in the baby care aisle and he was staring at the shelves full off stuffed animals and stroller toys.

"We're not pregnant yet," I looked with him, imagining the spare room decorated and full to the brim with toys. "We've only just done a test."

"I know. It might bring us procreating luck."

"Okay, you choose something. Nothing gender-specific. I need to get some new shampoo."

Thomas met me in the hair care aisle and I turned when I heard a thump in the trolley.

"What did you buy?"

He smiled. He was proud of himself.

"A patchwork blanket and..." he pulled something cream out from under the blanket. "A bunny comforter. I thought since we're eating like rabbits, it fits."

"I love you."

"You just want me for my shopping skills," he winked and threw his arm around me. "Love you, too."

I took the bunny off him and caressed the little square of blanket attached to it.

My phone rang and I pulled it from my bag, sighing when I saw the name on the screen. Thomas sighed, too, and took the trolley while I answered the call.

"Hi, Nina."

***

We waited with baited breath as the little white stick laid on the back of the bathroom sink. Thomas held my hand and we stared. And stared.

We sagged in disappointment when only one line appeared.

"Next month," I smiled weakly.

"Next month."

Thomas wrapped his arms around me and nuzzled into my neck.

***

I was running late. I was sitting in Thomas' office finishing off some things for Nina. I tried to get it done before he got out of the shower, but when I heard the remains of water drip down the pipe just outside the window, I knew I was caught. I wasn't supposed to be working. I'd had a chest infection for a couple of weeks and I was drained. Under Thomas' orders, when out of the office, I stepped out of the office; which meant he was not going to be happy that I was sitting in his chair and being sneaky.

I jumped when I felt him enter the room. The back of the chair moved when he held onto it and leaned down to kiss my bare shoulder. I had been getting ready to join him in the shower when Nina emailed me, so I had run downstairs naked.

"What are you doing?" He breathed, knowing full well what I was doing. He could see the screen without his glasses on.

"I just have to finish this." I coughed and he rubbed my back before moving round and sitting on the edge of the desk.

"I asked you to stop."

I rolled my head and sat back in the chair to look at him.

"I'm done, it's done. She's my boss, I can't say no."

"Yes, you can," he kissed my forehead, stood up and held out his hand. "Shift over, it's shower time. I put some eucalyptus oil in the shower. It'll clear your chest."

"Thanks, doctor."

I rose heavily from the chair and went to shower. I could tell by the tension in Thomas' body that he was mad, though he hid it well.

Forty Two

Something sweet, tender, romantic and real...That was what we had. And nothing, nothing, could compare to that.
February, 2011.

All I could see was the outline of Thomas' body when he placed my legs over his thighs and my back arched as he pulled me onto his lap. Cupping my face, his thumb traced my bottom lip before he replaced it with his mouth and sealed it over mine. I wrapped my arms around his neck and his fingertips tickled a trail down my back and to my hips.

He lifted me onto him, lowering my body onto his and gently easing into me, forcing gentle laments of pleasure to escape from us. My grip tightened, our tongues stroked and danced, sealing our connection. I felt whole. Thomas kept his hands on my hips, controlling my rhythm as I moved on top of him and sighed in tender bliss.

Our movements were slow, allowing our hands to explore as we conducted the sensual dance these nights created. Life had run away with us, but we would always have our chemistry, the hunger for each other that allowed us to shut the world out and consume each other.

Thomas lifted his hips as I rocked into him. I leaned back with my hands on the mattress behind me. We could see everything; every time he slid in and we lost ourselves in each other; every expression and gasp as the pleasure took control of all other sensations.

I shivered as Thomas rolled his hips, the intense power of his thrusts easing me ever nearer towards ecstasy.

No words were spoken; we simply watched each other and listened to every sigh, every moan, every ragged breath as we took each other.

He laid me back, locking my ankles at the bottom of his back, linked his fingers with mine and raised our hands above my head. Long, slow strokes had me pulsing around him, drawing him into the depths of my soul. My core tightened and I succumbed. I let my release crash over me, freeing me from my own mind. I tensed and tightened, encouraging him to follow me. He let go with a guttural groan and spilled into me, letting us escape to a world where only we existed.

Exhausted, Thomas collapsed next to me and pulled me into him. I didn't bother setting the alarm.

I closed my eyes and fell asleep in the arms of the man I loved.

Forty Three

He was kind of freaky. He was kind of an animal...I was unaware, but I was slowly coaxing the animal out of its cage. February 18th, 2011.

"Skye, can't you just leave it?"

Thomas ran his hands through his hair and groaned in exasperation. We'd just returned home from one of his work functions. I knew he was tired; the beer was wearing off, his stomach was probably growling with the need to be fed and, judging by the equally hungry growl rumbling low in his chest, so was his stronger, more demanding appetite.

I on the other hand, was antsy and I was frantically trying to ease it.

Thomas had held out his hands in the taxi on the way home, but I didn't want to play. I refused the gift, accepting that I'd pay for it later, one way or another, and left him to pay for the taxi while I went inside. And now I was battling with the cushions. It's what I did when I was restless. I couldn't control my emotions but I had control over the way the house looked.

"You know I can't."

I frantically arranged the cushions...and then rearranged them again. I couldn't get them to look right.

"Leave them."

"No."

I pulled them from the sofa and began placing them in a new arrangement.

"Are you trying to piss me off?"

"Piss you off?"

"Work me up, rile me. Whatever."

"What?" I stood up and saw him in the doorway with his feet shoulder width apart and his arms folded over his broad chest. "No."

Maybe. God, I loved that stance. It rendered me speechless, unintelligent…frazzled. Seeing him like that made my stomach flip and heat like a burning flame ready to explode into a flash tore through me.

"Tell me again like you mean it."

I stood my ground. I didn't want to play games…I didn't *think* I wanted to play games. I picked up a cushion and launched it at him. It bounced off his chest and sighed in defeat as it hit the floor with a huff. Yeah, the cushion knew where we were heading, too.

"I don't want to have sex with you."

He strode purposefully towards me. He knew. My denial held about as much conviction as a stripper refusing a raise.

I gasped as he gripped my hip and reared me back to the wall, forcing my breath to escape in a gust. The pictures fell from the sideboard as I gripped it for support. Thomas' hips pinned me to the wall. I was trapped when he grabbed my hands and held them against the wall by my sides.

"I don't believe you," he growled. "I know your game."

"You do?" I matched the aggression in his voice with a ferocity of my own.

I had been suffering with it all night; the palpitating ache, the searing erotic rage. I knew it and he knew it.

"Yes," he sucked my bottom lip, leaving it swollen and tingling when he pulled back and his eyes bore into mine. "You don't want to be caught. You want to be taken. You want me to fuck you so hard I send the tension into next week."

I whimpered.

"Admit it," he breathed as his teeth pulled at my ear. "Do you want me to fuck you senseless?"

"Yes."

I released a shaky groan when his hand slipped between us, pulled up my dress and a gentle stroke betrayed my efforts to conceal my arousal. I was soaked.

"See? You were going to deny it. You were going to go to bed aching for my dick but refusing to take what's yours."

"Yes," I crashed my head back.

"Why?" He pulled my underwear aside, and wasted no time diving through my drenched folds, filling me with two fingers while his thumb found my clit.

"I want you to take it," I hummed, rocking my hips into his hand.

Through the blood that roared in my ear and the quivering that quickly built in my core, I heard him growl; an unrestrained sign of primal, carnal delight. He snapped my underwear away and I watched his eyes darken as he tugged open his trousers. The button popped off, the zip tore and his rigid length replaced his thumb, the crown coaxing the nub to swell and pulse.

He shoved me up the wall, lifted me from the floor and I cried out as he pulled my legs tight around his waist, allowing himself to slam into me in one powerful move and he did fuck the tension into next week. Relentlessly.

Forty Four

Was I crazy? Was I that crazy girlfriend? I'd never felt more like a batshit crazy spinster…Was I a batshit crazy spinster?
March 19th, 2011.

Thomas had a 'work thing' on Saturday night. He usually said that when he planned to spend the night with Chaz and Joel. It almost always involved sport so, technically, he could get away with calling it a work thing. Beth and I planned to go out for dinner and few drinks.

Things were okay with her but, honestly, I was distracted. Having her around made me crave a family more than I ever thought possible. I'd slowly gone from nothing to having everything I ever wanted. Now all I wanted was to be a mother; to hold a bundle of innocence in my arms and know that Thomas and I would raise it together and love it forever. But it just wasn't happening.

And now Thomas was going away, I'd be home alone for the night and I would miss him.

"You'll remember what I said?"

Thomas dragged his weekend bag down the stairs and dropped it in front of the door.

"Yes. I'm the obsessive one, remember?"

He laughed and kissed the tip of my nose, "Humour me…What did I say?"

"Don't walk Buster in the dark, make sure all the doors are locked by sunset and switch off the downstairs sockets before I go to bed."

"That's my girl."

He kissed me between the eyebrows. I closed my eyes.

"I don't want you to go."

"I don't want to go, but it's work. It's just one night."

I could count the number of nights we'd been apart since I moved in on one hand. My Ikea furnished shoebox was no match for the four bedroom, three bath castle Thomas lived in. Okay, it wasn't a castle, but it had its own grounds and no nosey neighbours overlooking it. He'd been there three years when we met and he spent every evening and weekend renovating it until it was perfect. As far as I was concerned, it was our castle. We were living our fairy tale, only one of us was flying the coop for the night.

The last thing we needed was to be spending the night apart. In separate towns.

"Can't you stay? Isn't that one of the perks of being the boss?"

"Yes," he rolled his eyes, but couldn't hide the smile that played on his lips. "But it comes with the job, too. If I spend my days sitting behind a desk barking orders, I'll lose all respect and become detached."

I sighed. I knew he was right. You couldn't control what you didn't invest yourself in. I knew he had to go, I just didn't want him to.

"I know."

"I'll drive home first thing in the morning. We'll turn our phones off and do something. Just the two of us."

Perfect. We had spent so much time around people lately; colleagues at functions, Fran and Martin's new fortnightly dinners, time with our friends and dates with Beth and Jack. We barely had the time to enjoy each other. Our ivory tower had an open invitation.

The realisation of my dependency on him was a huge reality check. I had to let him go without making a fuss.

"Don't worry," he rubbed the top of my arms and pulled me into him. "I want to stay as much as you want me to. I like that you need me."

"You do?"

He nodded, the stubble on his chin tickling my forehead; he was still squeezing me and I was sure he smelled my hair.

"Yeah, it's an ego thing," he was trying to play it cool. "And I need you too."

"Hurry home, okay?"

"I'm already back."

He pulled my hair away from my face and gathered it at the back of my head. His lips brushed mine before he kissed me; tender yet firm. It was a kiss that both calmed and excited.

We walked to his car and he climbed in, shut the door and opened the window.

"I'll call you tonight, okay?"

I nodded and kissed him goodbye.

"I love you."

"I love you."

I watched as he drove away and headed inside to call Beth. I wanted to go out.

We were halfway through dinner when I reached into my bag for my phone and realised I had left it at home.

"Beth, we have to go."

"What?" she garbled a response with a mouthful of garlic bread.

"I've forgotten my phone and Thomas is supposed to call. We have to go."

"Just finish dinner. You can call him from mine when we're done."

I relented; I didn't trust Beth not to judge me if I told her how uneasy I felt. I panicked silently, my dinner forgotten.

I just didn't feel right.

I dropped Beth at her house and sped home. My phone was sitting on the counter in the kitchen where I left it and I snatched it up. Six missed calls from Thomas and as many voicemails. I hit call.

"Where have you been?" He answered as soon as the phone rang.

I felt better the second I heard his voice.

"I went for dinner with Beth and forgot my phone. I just got back."

"I was worried," he sighed and I imagined him running his hands through his hair. "Did you have fun?"

"Yeah," I lied. I couldn't tell him I'd been going crazy. "What are you doing?"

"Taking a break before it starts. Did you lock up?"

"It's still early."

"It's dark. Lock up."

"Yes, Sir."

I tried to keep the mood light, but it was anything but.

"Don't play. I'm not there to protect you if something happens."

"Geez, okay. I thought I was the crazy girlfriend."

"Well, I guess I'm the crazy boyfriend."

He was sulking. Great. The only downside to being with someone with a childish side was that he sulked like a teenager. I checked the back door and walked through the house to lock up the front.

"Why are you so miserable?" I asked.

"Because I want to be at home with you."

"Maybe a night apart is what we need."

"Seriously?" He was shocked. It sprung up my defences. "Are you playing the "we need a break" card?"

"No." We were heading for a fight. I felt the tension rolling over us like an approaching storm. "I don't want to be the crazy girlfriend."

"Intensity isn't insanity."

"There's a fine line."

"I can't do this. I have to work. I love you the way you are…we're crazy for each other."

"Yeah, well, you're not the one falling apart."

"Thanks for the trip to Guilt Gorge. You could have come with me."

"I wasn't invited. I don't even know where you are."

"Kent."

"What?"

That word. That place. It stopped my heart in its tracks and I felt the last remains of sanity slip away.

"Kent."

"Why didn't you tell me?"

"I didn't realise-" he trailed off.

"You didn't realise what?"

"Nothing," he spoke with soft caution. "Forget I said it."

"You didn't realise I had no emotional independence? You didn't realise it would only take me a few hours to miss you? You didn't realise I was Crazy Sarah number two?"

"I didn't say that."

"You didn't have to."

I hung up and stared at the screen.

I knew where he was and it hurt like a thousand daggers to the chest knowing he was there and I wasn't. I unlocked the front door and left the house.

Forty Five

Déjà vu...I should have felt the déjà vu.
March 19th, 2011.

I couldn't remember how I got there. I just saw darkness, a few street lamps that didn't give much away and a row of shops in the shadows. I climbed out of the car, ignoring the buzz in my pocket and slammed the door.

I didn't remember the drive that led me to where I was; I could have killed someone. I could have run myself off the road because I was in a trance, unable to deal with my own erratic mental state

Things had begun to spiral and that's why I flipped. They'd been spiralling slowly for weeks, waiting for the tailspin. It was the mother of tailspins.

I suddenly remembered walking out of the house after putting the phone down on Thomas. I didn't like him going away; I was afraid he wouldn't come back. He was right; he told me every time I snapped at him...it was an irrational fear, but I couldn't help it. He couldn't be there. The clock was ticking, I could feel it. I didn't know what it was counting down to but I felt each grain of sand as they fell.

We still hadn't conceived, my job was falling to shit because I was overworked and under-stimulated and I felt like we were stuck in our life; I wanted to take his hand and run from work, from home, from the guilt that I couldn't give him a child. Everything was perfect before we let people in and started planning the future. So I did run, only without Thomas and I couldn't, as I stood on the dark street alone, bring myself to answer his call.

One foot found its way in front of the other and a walk began; a walk with only one direction planned out, until I was standing in front of a black door and pounding my fist on the cracked paint.

"Password," a voice boomed from behind the door.

The only evidence of life was that voice and it sent a shiver down my spine.

I opened my mouth and let the gut-wrenching words roll from my tongue.

"Row, row, row your boat."

The door opened with a creak and I froze. My heart broke clean in half like my life had the last time I stepped over that threshold. The hallway smelled how I remembered it; like cheap air freshener and sweat. I remembered climbing the stairs before, with a mere percentage of the pain I felt in this moment. Why was I there? I should have been able to let Thomas be, but I just couldn't. Not there. Why did I continue to punish myself? That's what I was doing, with every step I took out into the open space, so full of bodies I couldn't see the walls…just the ring.

And the cage.

The cage my precious brother died in.

I stood at the top and looked down on the crowds. I remembered the fear of the unknown I felt all those years ago.

It froze me to the spot.

It stopped all hopes of oxygen entering my lungs.

Willing my body to turn proved pointless when the lights dropped, the crowds cheered and the music started as the MC entered through the door of the cage and into the ring.

"And noooww!" He announced, but his voice was lost to the white noise in my head.

I was nineteen again.

I was terrified.

But, like before, I was not alone.

I saw him.

Thomas was there with Chaz and Joel, and I saw his photographer and journalist next to them. He was working and I was in the tunnel of torment I'd been trying to ignore for so long.

He had his phone to his ear and the buzzing of mine continued. He clenched the hand that wasn't gripping his phone and chewed on his bottom lip; mine trembled as my heart sank and I ached to go to him. I wanted to be wrapped in his warm embrace; the only place I felt safe, but I couldn't move.

All thoughts of safety and surrender left my mind when the fighters made their way to the ring and all I could remember was the flash of green from Oliver's mouthguard, but no helmet. He would've lived without a few teeth. It was the punch to the back of the head that killed him.

The bell rang and my eyes fixated on the two men in the ring. Punches. Kicks. Grappling.

Cheers erupting from the crowds.

Pain.

Crippling pain.

Memories.

Blood boiling, stomach roiling memories.

Thomas.

I looked over to find him looking at me. He'd spotted me in a crowd of hundreds. Chaz waved; he must have thought I was meeting them there. That wasn't the plan. There was no plan.

Thomas stood and I backed away as he pushed through the sea of people. Another punch. Another cheer. Another step back.

My back collided with the front of someone and I turned to see a stoic bouncer with him arms folded, his eyes glued to the fight instead of looking at me. Keeping his gaze on the action, he reached out with one hand and shoved me backwards. I stumbled.

"Get your hands off her."

"No touching," the bouncer growled.

"Does she look aggressive to you?"

Thomas took a step towards him. Bad idea. He was probably an ex backstreet boxer; most of the bouncers in the circuit were…or used to be. Judging by the looks of things, it hadn't changed much since the last time I was there.

"No touching."

"Thomas, please," I begged, as he continued to square up to him. "Please, let's just go."

"No exit during fights."

The bouncer grunted and folded his steroid-enhanced arms. His co-bonehead laughed. They were goading Thomas. I knew they were allowed to use blunt force if 'necessary', which meant they could taunt him until he made the first move and wouldn't hesitate to kick the shit out of him.

"Open the doors."

I wretched at the sound. I had no control; my body quivered, my heart hammered; my skin fell cold as the voice wafted over my skin and froze me to the core. It had to be a nightmare. It couldn't be happening.

The bouncer nodded obediently, like I'd seen many others do before him and clicked the door open with a sneer.

I took off, running through the corridors until I was outside, sucking in the crisp air and gasping for more.

"Skye?"

Thomas. God, I was fucked. Catastrophically. Anyone who needed a quick fix of insanity could've jumped into my mind at that moment and had the ride of their life.

Standing up straight, I saw Thomas pulling on his coat. I hadn't even taken mine off. I was sweating; my entire body was on fire, yet my skin prickled with goosebumps.

"What are you doing here?"

"I don't know."

It was the truth, more or less. I didn't know *why* I was there; I just knew that I had to be.

"Give me your keys." I handed them to him and caught sight of my trembling hands. I was a mess; I could only imagine what I looked like. "Get in the car."

He opened my door and I fell in, shakily pulling my seat belt over me as he made his way round to the other side.

"Where's your car?"

"At the hotel."

He put the key in the ignition and the purr of the usually quiet engine echoed around the car as he pulled off.

Forty Six

I should have seen it coming. Impossible. I'd always been too wrapped up in the storm that tormented me. But I should have seen it.
March 19th, 2011.

"You've got to talk to me, Skye," he gripped the wheel with white-knuckle force. "What the hell was that?"

"I don't know," how was I supposed to talk to him when I didn't know what was going on? "I'm sorry."

"You reacted like that because I was there? I told you I was working. How did you know where to find me?"

"That place..." I took a shaky breath. "That's where Oliver died."

"Oliver was a fighter."

It wasn't a question. It was a realisation. Everything had just clicked into place.

"Yes," I bowed my head and picked at a piece of cotton on my jeans.

"Why didn't you tell me?"

"I don't know."

"Why?!" I flinched. He was so angry. His voice was guttural, shaky, and the vein in his neck thumped with pulse racing frustration. "What the hell were you doing there?"

"I don't know!" I cried. The tears fell and I couldn't stop them. I wanted him to understand the chaos in my mind, but even I couldn't make sense of it. "I didn't want you there...where Oliver died."

"This can't happen," He ground his teeth and continued to drive, pulling out onto the M25 and speeding up. "We can't fall apart because you're losing your mind."

"I'm not crazy."

"I didn't say that."

"You don't have to. You don't think I can feel the tension too? I honestly don't know how I get there, but I panicked. That doesn't mean we're falling apart."

"I just don't know what's going on with you. Why would you not tell me something like that?"

"I don't know, but we're *not* falling apart. It was just easier to shut it out."

I could see his anger had eased, but his frustration just grew. I could feel it bouncing back off him and keeping me on edge. I knew he just wanted to shake some sense into me; I did too. But I knew it wouldn't work.

"I just don't get it," he switched lanes and turned on the cold air. We were both seething. We were both angry. With me. "Why did you go in? Why didn't you turn around and go home? Why didn't you answer the damn phone and tell me you needed me?"

"I don't know. I didn't know I wasn't okay. I just needed to get to you."

"You didn't see the look in your eyes. I did. I saw it and you've kept that from me for years."

"I'm sorry." I had hurt him. I had kept something from him. We had always spoken. *Always.* He told me everything and I had denied him the most important truth. "I'm so sorry."

"Damn it, Skye, that's not good enough!"

He slammed his hands on the wheel and turned his head to look at me.

"Thomas!"

Forty Seven

Life. You blood sucking, soul destroying piece of shit…Take mine, I don't need it.
March 19th, 2011.

Glass. There was glass everywhere. I opened my eyes to see it covering my lap in little glittering clusters. It was in my hair. I lifted my fingers to my hair to comb it out. Warmth. I looked at my fingers. Blood.
Thomas.
I turned to him. He was quiet, slumped over the steering wheel.
"Thomas?"
I pulled him back and his head fell against the headrest. Blood poured from his nose; it ran down his jaw as it trickled from his ear.
He was wheezing, struggling to breathe as he turned his head and looked at me.
"Skye."
The words gurgled from his lips as he reached for me and wiped my own blood away with his thumb.
"Ssh," I choked. "We're going to be okay."
There was a bang on my window. Someone had stopped to help us. Headlights shone into the car from every direction.
"Help is on the way," someone's muffled voice came through the window and seeped into the non-existent windscreen.
I could feel the cold air rushing in through the hole, but I didn't take my eyes off Thomas.
"Skye," blood spat from his mouth as he coughed and took my hand.
"Don't talk. Help is coming."
He shook his head. His eyes were bloodshot and tears streamed from them. He was in so much pain.
"I love you…I'm sorry."

"Don't you dare," I whimpered. I tried with everything I had to hold it in. "Don't you dare apologise and don't tell me you love me again until we're in the hospital. We're going to be okay."

He coughed again and winced as blood fell from his mouth and soaked into his shirt. He was paling. His temperature was dropping. I felt it as his grip on me loosened.

"Squeeze, Thomas. Squeeze my hand."

I felt the twitch. He was trying.

"Just tell me," he rasped. "Tell me you love me."

"I love you. I love you with everything I have and all that I am. And I will continue to love you when we get out of this mess."

"Tell my parents," he choked. Each breath was getting harder. "Tell them I love them. Tell Ava I'm sorry and…and hug the boys."

"You can do it yourself," I used my teeth to pull my ring from my finger and slid it onto his blood stained little finger. "You promised. You promised you wouldn't leave me."

I could barely see his face through the tears that blurred my vision, but I kept my eyes on his.

"I'll never leave you."

His other hand reached for me. I reached for him. We were stuck. The tears poured until I could taste the salt and the metallic taste of blood.

"Where does it hurt?"

I tried to let go of his hand to feel for a bleed – I could try to stop it – but he squeezed my hand and tried to shake his head.

"It doesn't," another cough. More blood. "The only thing I feel is how much I love you." He tried to take a deep breath. He couldn't. I saw it then; he was suffocating. "You made…you made my life. You…you completed it."

"No," I sobbed. "Don't you dare."

I saw the flashing lights.

So many lights.

So much noise.

"They're here, Thomas. They're going to save you," I gripped his hand with both of mine and kissed it over and over. I prayed my pulse would kick start his. I could feel it fading.

"Don't leave me, Thomas."

He wheezed, "Never."

"Stay with me. Baby, fight with me. Please."

"Always."

The doors were wrenched from the car and strangers burst through our bubble.

"We're going to get you out," one of them said.

"Save her," Thomas sobbed and used all his might to breathe. More blood coated his chin. "Get her out...Save *her!*"

Someone strapped something around my neck. Hands slid under my body and pulled.

"No!" I screamed and gripped Thomas' forearm. "No! Please! Don't!"

I held onto Thomas until I was torn from him and pulled from the wreckage.

Through the sirens and whirring tools and voices, all I heard was Thomas tell me he loved me.

Forty Eight

No words. I had no words.
March, 2012.

I pulled the patchwork blanket, the one we had bought for our future baby, around my shoulders as I stared out of the window. Buster rested his head on my lap and I dropped my hand to his head.

One year. It had been one year since I died in the passenger seat of my car.

The blood pumped through my veins.

The oxygen made its way into my lungs because I had no choice but to let it.

But I had died one year ago with the man who owned my heart.

I didn't want to live without Thomas.

I quit my job and completed an online course in proofreading. I worked from home, accepting files from strangers and taking their money for changing punctuation marks and correcting syntax errors, and then I emailed the file back. There was no interaction, no personal relationships, no coffee meetings to discuss my changes. I switched off the night Thomas died and my last ounce of self-worth was used up when I passed his message onto his family, remembering the terrified expression on his face as he spoke it. He wasn't ready to die. He was afraid of death because we hadn't done everything we wanted to do. He was afraid of dying because it shouldn't have been him losing his life with every beat of his heart that allowed more blood into his lung. His rib had broken upon impact with the central reservation and pierced his lung. He drowned in his own blood. The internal bleeding was so severe by the time he got to hospital, that there was nothing they could do.

It was my fault. If I hadn't lost my mind and gone searching for the past when I had everything I ever needed in my present, Thomas would have still been alive, blowing raspberries on my neck while I tried to work, or combing his fingers through my hair as we laid in the sun.

But he wasn't. He was gone and I was a prisoner in our house, surrounded by ghosts and the reminders of what could have been. They say the good die young, but I didn't believe it. The good deserve to live. The good deserve the precious gift of life they've been given. Thomas deserved to live, and it was my fault he couldn't.

Beth came by every weekend and Jack came with her to do things around the house that Thomas would have done. He mowed the lawn and fixed whatever had broken while Beth cleaned. A few months after the funeral I went to the DIY store and bought new door handles with locks. I had Jack fit them and when they'd gone, I walked around the house; I said goodbye to the games room, the wet room, the office and our bedroom before shutting and locking each door.

I slept on the sofa or in the spare room and I worked from the lounge while listening to the playlist Thomas had made me.

Even after a year, Jen, Amanda and Penelope still stopped by. They took it in shifts to bring me food and watch me eat it. They took such pride in the meals they brought, but it could have been anything. I ate it to keep me alive, but I couldn't taste anything.

Sometimes they'd all come together, the girls and Beth, and talk about their days, just to get me to interact. I stared off into space and shut them out; I didn't want the sound of their voices to erase the memory of Thomas'.

When they left, I'd switch on his phone and watch the videos we'd made; silly videos of us singing to each other, or arguments that quickly turned into a tickle fight because we couldn't stand to be mad at each other. I couldn't bring myself to watch our intimate videos. I craved his hands on me, or linked with mine as we made love. I craved his smell. I craved how I smelled after we'd been together. I just missed *him*; it didn't even cover how I felt but that's all I had.

I couldn't breathe when I thought about living out the rest of my days without him. I wasn't living; I just existed. But I didn't want to. Every time my breath halted and the pain and regret overpowered my will to live, I hoped the venomous guilt I deserved to wallow in would stop my heart and allow me to slip away and find my beloved.

Maybe the good did die young. If they did, I would spend long years alone and I deserved every heartbreaking, soul crushing minute of it.

"Is there anything I can do?" Beth asked as she and Jack prepared to leave.

"No, thank you."

"I'll pop in tomorrow."

"It's okay," My voice was a drone, a monotone. "I don't need anything."

"I'll send one of the girls, then."

"Beth, I'm fine."

She made me jump when she spoke minutes later. I thought they'd left.

"You're a fighter, Skye. You'll get through this," she kissed the top of my head. "I love you."

"Me too."

She knew I couldn't say the words, so she gave my shoulder a soft squeeze and they left.

"What are we going to do, Buster?"

He whimpered and nuzzled into my hand for a stroke.

I *was* a fighter. I always had been.

Not anymore.

What was the point in pulling on the gloves and climbing into the ring when you had nothing left to fight for?

Forty Nine

I didn't have my happily ever after. My fairy tale had come to a sickening end. I couldn't be the reason someone else suffered the same fate.
March 7th, 2012.

There was a knock at the door. I opened my eyes and squinted when the bright light invaded them. I heard a voice outside. I closed my eyes again. They would go away.

"Skye?"

I jumped and fell off the sofa when I heard Ava's voice. She was standing at one end and I was in a tangle on the floor at the other.

"How did you get in?" I asked as I got up. I hadn't heard her come in.

"Beth told me where the spare key was."

"Great. Sorry, Ava."

I wasn't apologising for letting her in; I didn't want anyone and if she had been speaking to my sister she knew that already. I was apologising for my state. I pulled my tearstained t-shirt of Thomas' – the one I lived in – to my knees.

She nodded her head towards the kitchen and I reluctantly followed her.

"Coffee?" she filled the kettle as I slumped on the stool.

"No thanks," she took two cups from the cupboard anyway. "You came here from Jersey?"

"I left the boys with Kevin. They're going to have some boy time. They're camping in the garden tonight."

"Sounds nice." I mumbled, trying to squash the thought that Thomas and I would never do that with our own children. "But why are you here?"

"I've been speaking to Beth."

I knew it, "And?"

She placed my coffee in front of me and I wrapped my hands around the cup for warmth. I was always cold.

"And we think you should get away for a while."

"I don't need an intervention, Ava."

"I know," she sat opposite me and I pulled away as she reached for my hand. "You've been fighting on your own for too long. It's time to tag someone else in."

"I'm fine."

Of course I wasn't fine, but Ava had lost her brother. I knew how that felt. There was nothing that compared to the way she was feeling and I couldn't wallow in self-pity in front of her.

"Thomas wouldn't want you to be fine. He would want you to live."

"He would hate me for taking his life. He would wish it was me instead of him."

I told everyone, anyone who would listen, everything about the night of the crash. I told them to push them away. I wanted them to hate me as much as I hated myself, but it had the opposite effect. It made them pity me more, which made me hate myself more than I ever thought possible.

"Do you really believe that?" She cocked her brow just like Thomas did – used to do.

"It's what I choose to believe."

"He would want you to live and you know it," I shook my head to shut her up, but I knew she was right. Thomas has said the same thing about Oliver's death. "He would want you to do everything you planned to do together."

"He always said he wanted to watch me," I told her as her words began to sink in. "He said he never saw how much I loved him because he was distracted by how much he loved me. But I can't."

"Sounds like my brother. He was such a charmer," she grabbed my hand before I had a chance to move away again. "Show him. He can see it now. Show him how much you love him by living for him…or two lives were lost that night."

I nodded to satisfy her, but I didn't believe it. We didn't have two lives; we had one, and it had gone with him. I had to learn to live alone again.

"Besides," she smiled weakly through her own grief. "Your sister is waiting for permission to get married."

I gasped. Beth was supposed to be planning her wedding, not babysitting me. She had put it on hold for me and I hadn't even noticed. I was selfish. How had I not noticed?

"You said I should get away?"

"We're all going away. Today. It's booked and paid for. You, me, Beth and the girls."

"Where are we going?"

"Mexico."

I nodded. Thomas always wanted to go to Mexico.

***

The girls looked at me like I was an alien when we met them at the airport. The only time they'd seen me in the last year was when they sat in my house, dragged me to the supermarket or when we walked Buster around the lake under my cloud of depression.

Beth hugged me when Ava and I climbed out of the taxi with our suitcases.

She held me at arm's length.

"I heard Thomas tell you once that he knew what you needed," I felt the lump rise in my throat. I wanted to go home. "Will you let go and trust him to guide you?"

I nodded, "Only if you promise me one thing."

"Anything."

"Promise me you'll plan your wedding and let me help. Promise me you'll walk down the aisle and marry Jack."

She hesitated, but I knew she was exactly how I felt. I'd never plan my wedding. I'd never marry the man of my dreams.

That girl was gone.

"I promise."

Fifty

Was it okay to feel? Was it okay to smile? I'd never love again. I didn't want to…But could I smile and know that Thomas was smiling with me?
March 8th, 2012.

Mexico was hot. So hot. For the first time since the air gushed in through my smashed windscreen, I wasn't cold. I laid in the sun and closed my eyes. I laid in silence while the girls talked around me, planning dinner or an excursion.

"Jet skis!" Someone shouted. "Jet skis seventy dollars!"

I sat up and saw a little Mexican man parading the beach with a sign reading "Jet skis – one day hire".

I looked around and saw them all lined up around an inflatable jetty not far along the beach.

"Here!" I threw my arm in the air and caught his attention. He skipped excitedly over to us.

"You want to ride a jet ski?" Ava asked as I pulled some money from my bag. I ignored the overly comforting tone in her voice and handed Mexican Man his money.

"Gracias."

The assistant gesticulated heavily with his hands as he began explaining how to use the jet skis. I strapped the Velcro around my wrist, pulled on the throttle and shot off.

I'd ridden a jet ski before, in Jamaica with Thomas. I concentrated on the swish of the water as I remembered our holiday…

My hands were wrapped around his waist, my cheek pressed to his back. We laughed as we rode the waves and the adrenaline pumped wildly through our veins. I loved the feel of the purring engine, the wind in my hair, Thomas flexing as he steered us in donuts. And I loved the feel of the sun beaming down on us, burning with my love for the man who had whisked me away to the Caribbean one week after I confessed that I wanted to make love under the stars.

Beth was right. Ava was right. Being surrounded by the ocean gave me time to think. Thomas *would* want me to live and he would live it with me. I had to believe that. I had three of us to live for now. Oliver, Thomas and myself. I had three lives in the hands that were squeezing the handlebars of the jet ski and I couldn't waste them.

Fate had been fucking me over my whole life. Fate had been controlling me. What was the point in fighting, slugging the weight and pulling the punches, if I was never going to win?

I was going to fuck fate right back, and hard. I was going to teach it not to mess with Skye the Skillet. I was going to control my fate. Once again, I had to fight to survive. Fate could either submit and give me a break or fight back.

The only way I'd win this was to try. To live. To hope.

The old me was gone. I had to shut out the past, lock it away and fight. I had to survive.

Fifty One

Magic.
April 19th, 2014.

It was the night before my sister's wedding. Her dress was hanging from the wardrobe in her hotel room, the rollers were firmly in her hair and she was tucked up in bed, ready to marry the man of her dreams. I was happy for her; her husband-to-be was a great man and I knew he would make her a happy woman. They had both had their fair share of crazy exes and had found each other amongst the madness.

I made my way downstairs to the bar; I planned to have a quick nightcap, head up to bed, sleep and be ready and alert to perform my sister-of-the-bride duties the next day.

I ordered a large brandy as I sat on the stool at the bar. The bartender handed me a snifter of Courvoisier and I swirled the liquid around to coat the glass, inhaling the memories as I breathed in the scent. I looked around me as I took my first sip and noticed I was alone. It wasn't uncommon for me to be by myself, it was how I lived my life now.

I closed my eyes and inhaled as a soft breeze blew in through the open doors that lead to the hotel gardens; the smell of lavender, jasmine and the blossom on the trees heightened my senses, making me acutely aware of the warm glass in my hand and the soft chiffon covering my body. Unexpected butterflies began a sensual dance in my stomach.

I stood from the stool and made my way to the gardens. Something in the way my mind and body reacted to the light spring breeze called to me, compelling me to step out.

The outside was as baron as the inside, void of life except for the flowers that lined the pathway and the trees that swayed around the bandstand where my sister would soon recite her vows.

The breeze played a hypnotic symphony as it swirled around me; it lifted my dress so the cool air could tickle the tops of my legs and swish my dark hair around my face, bringing my attention to the warm flush on my cheeks. It pulled me further into the garden. My feet took light steps along the path; my mind had no control over the direction they took. I simply allowed the strange magic to guide me. I didn't fight this time. I didn't want to.

I reached the bandstand and counted the three steps as I took them up to the platform, set my glass down and curled my hands over the cold, smooth surface of the railing. I inhaled the leafy, woody scent of the trees surrounding me.

My eyes fluttered shut, just for a second, to bask in the surreal calm that washed over me.

I opened them again quickly when I heard footsteps.

A dark figure emerged from the trees and stopped at the threshold of the forest beyond. I was overwhelmed by the rush of something unfamiliar as the tall frame of the unknown man moved closer.

I was frozen to the spot but unafraid.

The man was a stranger. He had no name. He had no face; it was hidden by the dark shadows of the trees. But he had a power; a power so strong I had no choice but to succumb to it, to let it overpower me. All I could do was let the intensity of his presence pull me in, and flourish in the effects as the soft heat that had been forgotten for so long began to swim through my veins.

He stepped up onto the platform and my body instinctively turned to him as he stopped opposite me and leant back on the railing.

I walked towards him.

My destination was decided.

Fate had made a move.

The charge in the atmosphere sucked more air from my lungs with each step I took until I was breathless and standing inches from him. His presence drew me in, pulled me closer and I was the helpless little moth edging ever nearer to the smouldering flame. I was no longer the Skillet; I was closing in on one.

My mind separated from my body as he reached out, took my hand and encouraged me to take the final step. My body met his; his hard, mine soft, and we shared the heat – I warmed his and he fuelled mine. It passed between us like electricity. I physically felt the spark that drew my mouth to his, and my heart leapt as if it had been shocked when our lips touched.

I didn't know him, this stranger who had captivated me. But I felt like I did. I was somebody else the second he touched me. As his soft, gentle kiss sent bursts of adrenaline, desire and longing through me, I was transported to a place where I knew him. For a moment in time our souls were joined as one, the chemistry so strong it was as if we were one person living in two bodies and I was no longer in the garden. I didn't know where. I didn't know when. I only knew that I was far, far away and I felt like I had been there before…

Revival

(Twisted #2)

Sometimes life is shit. In fact, it's always shit. For people like me, at least.

What hope do you have when you lost everything before you knew what it meant to have it?

That happened to me at just five years old. It happened again at twenty-five. If that was the pattern, I dreaded what was going to happen when I hit forty-five. Hell, maybe God would finally do me a favour and put me out of my misery before I reached it.

You know that age old saying, "life is too short"? Yeah, well, mine was too long. I hadn't lived a life; I'd been forced to stop over in Hell and they forgot to tell me my plane back to normalcy was ready for take-off.

They could have told me my plane was delayed because I was being upgraded to first class. Maybe if they had, I would have done something to earn it. I really wanted to deserve it.

But I was that poor, unfortunate soul. I was that five-year-old boy stuck in the past, punishing the world for the life I lived.

My story? Yeah, why not?

This is me…Cut Throat Curtis.

Rebecca Sherwin

Acknowledgments

First and foremost, the most important acknowledgment has to go to my son, Alfie. We're a team – I do this not only for me, but for him. To show him that dreams come true. Just 18 months ago, I was too afraid to do this; to put myself out there. But it is watching him grow, raising him, teaching him, encouraging him in everything he does, that has allowed me to grow, to learn, to dream with him. It is the love I feel for him; a love so strong no words can describe, that has given me the strength to tell stories – to try to portray a love that is even a fraction of what I feel for him.

To my muse, thank you for giving me this story. If I didn't know you, I couldn't have written it and connected with it as strongly as I have. The parts of you that you have allowed me to see went into this story, so thank you for the tenderness and protection, the naughty and the nice, the guarded and the open, the dirty, the flirty, and everything in between. No limits, no expectations – just an island. Our island. You, Tiger, are something else.

To Paula Radell. Thank you, BB! I heart you hard. We have worked tirelessly on this project. You have done so much for me that "thank you" doesn't even begin to convey the gratitude and honour I feel to have you in my life. No getting rid of me now! You are a diamond. We are a team, nothing will change that. To many more sleepless nights, virtual tubs of ice cream, bottles of wine, hugs and tears.

To Catherine Scott, my right arm, my walking virtual calendar, my friend. Thank you for reading my stuff when it's nothing but scribbles and jibberish filled with typos and "wtf does that mean?" moments. Thank you for taking over and giving me a break. Thank you for sending me to write, and keeping me motivated. As you often tell me, "next step greatness".

To my beta readers:

To Mary E Palmerin : A great writer and lady. A great mother and dreamer. A great friend. Thank you.

To Edward A Stanbridge : Thank you for always making me smile. Thank you for always offering words of encouragement and for fixing my medical 'glitches'. Thank you for reading again and again and never getting bored. Thank you for being you.

To Jen Lynn : You shocked my socks off with your first message. I'll never forget your reaction or the smile I wore for hours afterwards. Thank you for reading and popping up in my messages asking when you can buy!

To Caroline Rizzi and Jennifer Juers : You were the first readers to criticise the things I couldn't change. I had to put my foot down and keep the story as it was – the voices told me to!

To my Ravishing Readers:
You ladies rock! You are the chocolate chips in my cookie dough, the cherry on my ice cream sundae, the awesomeness that floats my boat daily.

To Laurie Schmidt Lee, Violet Goodwin Smith, Kerry-Ann Bell, Tanya Zarb, Anne Morillo, Chelsea Barnes, Brittany Alexander, Renee McKinney, Louise Hands, Styliani Congi and the other amazing ladies who volunteer to help promote me and my stories.

I love each and every one of you.

To the 43 authors and bloggers who donated something to the pre-release giveaway, gave up their time to host a takeover during the pre-release party, and offered their words of wisdom and support, thank you so much.

And to the 57 bloggers who volunteered to take part in the pre-release activities, sharing updates, posting the cover, the trailer, the giveaways, the links and every little, fun thing we sent you to try and get as many people engaged and having fun as possible, thank you so much.

And to my readers. The world is lonely for authors who have no readers. Keep reading, keep believing and know that dreams come true, fairy tales exist and true love can last forever.

Rebecca Sherwin

Thank you for taking the time to pick up my work and an extra-large dose of love if you've made it this far. I'm almost done – not long now, I promise.

Continue to support your favourite authors, continue to explore their fictional worlds and introduce yourself to new ones, and please consider leaving a review for every book that has you hooked, leaves you breathless and allows you to escape to another world.

Contact

I'd love to hear from you. There is no question too small, no request too big.

You can find me on Facebook, either by searching my name and sending a friend request, or:

*"Like" my page for regular news and updates on my WIPs and upcoming releases, giveaways, what I'm reading and where you can find me during takeovers and events
https://www.facebook.com/rebeccasherwinauthor
* Follow me on Twitter
https://twitter.com/RRSherwin
*Follow my blog
https://www.rebeccasherwin.wordpress.com
*Find me on Goodreads
https://www.goodreads.com/RebeccaSherwin
*Or send me an email
missrsherwin@gmail.com

The release of Survival (Twisted #1) and all following releases by Rebecca Sherwin, will be sponsored and hosted by Passionate Promotions, and represented by Paula Radell.

You can find more information by clicking the following links:
http://passionate-promotions.com/ or
https://www.facebook.com/PassionatePromos
and
http://curlupandread.com/

Come and support the Survival #Fabulous43

Celebrate and support the 43 authors and bloggers who offered their support, time and donations to the release of Survival. Adopt an Author with Passionate Promotions . Introduce yourself to a new author and spread the love!
http://passionate-promotions.com/

One final big thank you to everyone on this journey with me. I hope you enjoy the ride.

Happy reading!

Made in the USA
Charleston, SC
08 February 2016